I THEE TAKE

TO HAVE AND TO HOLD DUET BOOK TWO

NATASHA KNIGHT

Copyright © 2021 by Natasha Knight

All rights reserved.

No part of this book may be reproduced in any form or by any electronic or mechanical means, including information storage and retrieval systems, without written permission from the author, except for the use of brief quotations in a book review.

1

CRISTIANO

Six men lie on the ground at the front of the house, all but two shot execution style. The two are riddled with bullets. They were taken by surprise. The others were rounded up. They saw death coming.

"The front door was open when we got here," Antonio says.

I should have left him with her. Why didn't I leave him?

"Any of their soldiers among the dead?" my uncle asks.

Antonio shakes his head.

We were ambushed. Betrayed again. No one knew this house even existed. Even if they did, no one knew she was here. No one but the men who were here with her. Who are now dead.

All except for one.

"Where's Alec?" I ask. He's the lone survivor. He called it in a few hours ago.

"Kitchen."

I look beyond the house to the mountains. Turn around to the ocean. They drove right up. Killed the men at the checkpoints and continued straight to the house.

Betrayed.

Again.

I turn to my uncle who has remarkably not puked at the sight of the bloodbath, both outside and inside the house. Maybe I don't know him as well as I think.

Inside is decidedly worse, the blood marking the walls and furniture. I'm taken back in time, back a full decade to another massacre.

The other half dozen men and the kitchen girl lie dead. Shot in the back of the head execution style like the others.

"Fuck."

The bedroom doors stand open and from here I see the rumpled bed, see the shards of glass from the whiskey bottle I'd smashed against the wall. The bathroom light is on, too.

At least she's not dead. They didn't kill her. Anything is better than dead.

"Cris," Alec starts, rising from his seat, but wincing and falling back down to the chair.

I look him over but can't tell how much of the

blood is his and how much is from the others. What strikes me most isn't that. It's his expression. The tears he's trying hard not to shed.

The last time I saw a grown man cry was when my father watched his wife degraded before his eyes.

My jaw tenses, my gut twists.

I go to him. "Are you okay?"

"I should be dead."

Why aren't you? I don't ask.

"He'll be fine. Out of commission for a while, but fine," the doctor who stitched me up just days ago says. Lately, it seems I singlehandedly keep his mortgage paid. "Can't work this arm for a while and he'll need a cast for his leg."

"Who were they?" I ask Alec.

"Mexican soldiers. Her uncle led them."

Jacob De La Cruz. I'd seen him just hours ago. Ordered him to arrange a meeting with that fuck Felix Pérez.

"Was she hurt?"

He doesn't quite look at me.

I grip his hair, force his face to mine. He needs to man up. I made a mistake trusting him to protect her.

"Did. They. Hurt. Her?"

"She was hunched over when they dragged her out," he pauses. "Naked," he adds in a barely audible whisper.

It's hard to swallow. I can't put a finger on the

thoughts and emotions turned to physical sensation inside me. Blood pounds against my ears. A burning hot rage followed by the cold fear of loss. Of losing someone else. Losing her.

My dream comes back to me, that scene again. Scarlett in my mother's place. Scarlett calling for me. Calling for me to help her. It was no coincidence.

"I figure if I'm drunk enough, it won't hurt as much."

I release him and walk into the bedroom. Glass crunches under my shoe. I look down only to see the wedding band I ripped from her finger.

I called her a whore. I almost hit her.

"I figure if I'm drunk enough, it won't hurt as much."

Won't hurt *as much*. It had struck me when she'd first said it. Not a virgin, no. How badly did Marcus Rinaldi hurt her? Did he do more than she let on? And was her uncle lying when he told me that story of how her brothers humiliated her? Wouldn't let Rinaldi touch her until after the wedding?

I shake my head, run a hand through my hair and bend to pick up the wedding band. I'd dropped it on the bed after forcing my mother's ring from her finger.

Fuck.

Fuck me.

No. It's not me who's fucked. It's her and I'm the asshole who let it happen.

I see the blood then. Not much but it's there on the terra cotta tile. A deep red stain against the rusty orange. It comes off the ring when I smear my thumb over it. I slip the gold band onto my pinkie finger. It only goes to the first knuckle. She's just a little thing. No match for the men who came for her.

"She was hunched over when they carried her out. Naked."

Did he touch her? Jacob? Would he have touched her?

"No." I pocket the ring and walk into the bathroom. If I go down that road, I will not be able to function.

This is where they surprised her. She must have been in the bath. Maybe trying to make sense of my accusation on our wedding night.

The tub is still mostly full and there's a lot of water on the floor. A towel lies discarded a few feet away. If I know Scarlett, they must have dragged her out of the tub kicking and screaming. She's a fighter. A survivor.

She'll survive until I can get to her.

She has to.

"Cristiano," my uncle calls, tucking his phone into his pocket.

"I want Jacob De La Cruz," I say. "Alive."

"Too late."

"What?"

"His body was found at some docks near Genoa."

"Genoa? That's what? Seven hours away?"

"Chopper should be here..." we both hear the sound at the same time. "Now."

"Where are Marcus and Felix?" I ask, as he and Antonio flank me on our way outside.

"Don't know yet. I put men on it," Antonio says.

The chopper lands, sending up a dust storm. I turn to Antonio. "Get Alec back to the house. I want you to watch him but don't alert him to anything. Put a man you trust on him. I want to know who he talks to. If he makes any calls. Understand?"

"Yes, sir." He's probably thinking the same thing I am. Why is Alec alive when they made sure everyone else was dead?

"Are you going home or coming with me?" I ask my uncle.

"I'm coming with you."

I nod and the two of us, along with a handful of soldiers, head toward the chopper.

My uncle stops me a few feet away. "You should have told me this is where you wanted to spend your wedding night," my uncle says. He has to raise his voice to be heard over the whirring of the blades.

"You'd try to talk me out of it."

"And for good reason. Why didn't you tell me? Even about the church?"

I consider my response. How much I want to give away. "You met with him," I say, finished with games. I've been finished with them since I woke up from the coma. Time has become more valuable. And I'm fucking tired.

Both eyebrows climb up his forehead. "Met with who?"

"Rinaldi."

"What?"

"Three years ago. On the balcony at the opera. I didn't even know you liked opera, Uncle." I study his face as I say it, laying out my cards, watching for any tells.

"What the fuck are you talking about?"

"I have a photo. Several. You and him, in a private and very heated discussion."

He studies me as closely, left eye narrowing infinitesimally. Then he laughs, just a quick burst of air as he shakes his head.

"It was a charity event. I'd been invited for my contribution. I can't dictate who the opera allows in and who they bar from entry, now can I?"

"So, you just coincidentally happen to be there at the same time as the man who murdered your brother, your sister-in-law, your niece and nephews? And you're able to hold a conversation with him knowing he's responsible? Knowing what he did to my mother?" That last part I force out, blocking the emotion that wants to worm its way into my words.

"What exactly are you accusing me of?"

"I don't know, Uncle."

"Where is this photo? How did you get it?"

"Doesn't matter. What were you talking about?"

"Quite honestly, I was taken by surprise when he, his soldiers, and those two Cartel brothers arrived at the box where I sat with the president of the charity. He came to pour salt into the wound, Cristiano. My anger got the better of me. I told him in no uncertain terms that one day, I would kill him."

"This lasted seven minutes?" The time was stamped on the photos.

"How dare you!"

"Look around you, Uncle. I was betrayed tonight. Again."

"And you think it was me? I didn't even fucking know where you were!" he pauses, glances around then lowers his voice. "Have you thought of Alec? Have you wondered how he managed to survive considering they made sure no one else did? The rest were killed execution style. No room for error when you have a fucking bullet in your head. Have you considered maybe it was him?"

"I consider everything," I say, somehow calm. "I have to. What else were you talking to Rinaldi about at the opera? Seven minutes is a long fucking time."

"I already told you. And if you doubt that I was as impacted by the murders of your family, then you're having a brain hemorrhage." He leans in close, pokes his finger against my chest. "Remember who saved your fucking life."

"Yeah, I remember. Dante."

"No, not Dante. He found you. I'm the one who made sure you were kept safe and protected while you couldn't defend yourself. *I* made sure you were taken care of, made sure you were out of sight until you were strong enough to stand on your own, to take back what was stolen from you and to avenge your family. You think Dante didn't want to go after them? You think I didn't want revenge? *I* protected him too. Saved his life too when he'd have thrown it away going after those fuckers. I knew all along we needed to wait for you. We couldn't take that from you, and that's the truth of it. But that doesn't mean I don't feel anything but hate for the family who killed my family."

I look beyond him to the waves of the ocean. I scrub my face, take a deep breath. It makes sense what he's saying.

The tattoo I scribbled badly on my arm throbs. My uncle's name. But if I look at him now, if I recall how he looked when he told me about last night, he was as surprised as I. And he's my own blood. My father's brother.

"Look, it's been a stressful few days. Scarlett's missing. I can guess who has her. You're under a lot of pressure. And I haven't helped when it comes to her. I know that. But believe me, Cristiano, I have no ulterior motive. You're the closest thing I have to a son. I'd never betray you."

I nod. It's all I can do. Right now, I have to get

Scarlett back. That's my first priority. All this I'll process later.

"Let's go," I say.

We walk in silence the rest of the way to the chopper and climb inside. The pilot lifts off the ground as soon as we're inside and I think about the last time we were in the chopper heading to my wedding.

How things change in a matter of hours. Minutes. Seconds.

How life turns upside down and inside out, spitting out what's left of us after it's chewed up everything that matters.

2

SCARLETT

Murmurs and quiet whimpers are the sounds I hear. The smell is dank, like sweat and something else, something rotten. When I'm jostled violently, those whimpers swell to a joint scream followed a few moments later by the sounds of someone retching.

I blink. Turn my head. My neck is sore, my shoulders, back and arms aching. I groan, try to bring my hand to my face but my wrists are bound behind my back. As my eyes open and the room comes into focus, I remember why.

I remember Marcus. Remember my uncle.

And Marcus killing my uncle.

I move backward through time and memory, remembering farther back to the room at that house. My bath. Cutting my foot on the shards of glass from the bottle Cristiano destroyed.

Our wedding night.

Cristiano accusing me of being a whore on our wedding night.

Something inside me twists but I don't linger because there's another one of those swells and panic grips me. I struggle to sit up just as we crash down and water sprays the windows, splashing through the one where the glass is missing. We're on a boat. A stinking, old, decrepit boat.

The women around me scream as I take it all in.

The stench. It almost makes my nostrils burn. Dirty mattresses line the floor, two or three women taking up each one. I look at their faces. Some can't be older than fifteen. Sixteen. I'm not sure who looks more terrified, though.

Some are quiet, staring ahead wide-eyed. Some are sobbing. Many have bruises on their faces, or on bits of exposed skin. Almost none of us are wearing shoes I realize.

"You okay?" the voice to my right croaks.

I look over at the girl. At twenty-two I must be one of the oldest ones in here. I nod to her, and she holds up a bottle of water. It's almost empty.

I lick my lips, nod.

She stretches her arms out to me. She's bound too, but her wrists are in front of her.

I drink a sip of the lukewarm, stale tasting water. "Thank you."

She can't be more than sixteen, I think, and

beneath the dirt and bruises and fear, she's beautiful.

"Are *you* okay?"

Tears spill down her cheeks. "I want to go home," she says with a noticeable accent.

My eyes fill up looking at her. Looking at all of them. I feel responsible for them. Like this is my fault. Like this is something I need to somehow fix.

I shiver and she reaches behind me with her bound wrists, tugs at something. I look back at it. It's a man's jacket.

She pulls it over my shoulders, the lining cool against my skin as I lean back against the wall. "Thank you." With my next breath, I smell the subtle scent of a familiar aftershave just beneath that of vomit and urine and fear.

"Where are they taking us?" I ask the girl sharing my mattress.

She shakes her head. "We've been on the boat for a while. And before that, the truck. I don't know how long it's been anymore."

Is Cristiano looking for me? Does he know what's happened? And who was the man with Marcus? The one who told him to cover me up. The man whose jacket I'm wearing.

"Where are you from?" I ask her.

"Croatia. Those two are from Croatia too. The others I don't know."

"How did they take you?"

"I was walking home from school. It was the middle of the afternoon. Bad things don't happen in the light." Her voice breaks and she starts to sob again.

"What's your name?"

"Sonia," she manages.

"Sonia. It's okay. It'll be okay."

Neither of us believes this lie but I can't not tell it.

A door slams against the wall of the room, metal clanging against metal. Startled, I gasp, my head snapping to the man standing in the doorway. It's the one from the dock. The fat one who cut the restraints at my ankles.

The women cower away as if one entity.

The man enters and from behind him follow another three, all with leering eyes, reeking of alcohol and days-old sweat.

But the one who frightens me the most is the last one to appear at the door. The one who looks clean. The handsome one.

I know he's the cruelest of the lot.

Marcus sneers as he looks in my direction and I remember how he shot my uncle. I wish I could wipe my face because I know I didn't imagine the blood that splattered it, but I'm not sure if I really feel it or if it's my mind playing tricks on me.

The men fan out, moving swiftly as they scan the

room. They look at something on the wrist of each of the girls before taking their pick.

The screams start then but all it takes to shut that down is the big one backhanding a girl so hard that her whole body spins and she slams face-first into the wall. I hear a crack and she drops to the floor of the boat. She's unconscious or dead. I can't tell. Broken for sure.

The screams become whimpers then as the men get back to what they came in here for.

I open my mouth to speak, to make them somehow stop, but one of the men grips my arm then and hauls me to my knees. I'm flipped over so I'm lying face down on the filthy mattress.

The girl beside me screams as I feel his hands on me, but then there's a sound, someone grunting, and I'm hauled to sit upright again.

"Not that one," Marcus says. "No one touches that one." He runs a hand gently over my cheek then grips my jaw so hard he's about to shatter it.

"No one but you?" I manage through gritted teeth.

"Not yet," he says, eyes darkening. "But it's coming."

He lets go of my jaw. In my periphery, I see the others moving behind the women, hear them grunting as the women whimper and sob. I don't want to look, but I know I have to. I have to catalog each of their faces for later. For when I can kill these men. For when I can free the women.

"You like the show?" Marcus asks me. "Is that what turns you on?"

I turn my gaze to him and spit the biggest spitball I can manage onto his face. It hits his right eye and smears down to his cheek. "Only monsters are turned on by this."

He wipes off my spit and looks like he's about a second away from murdering me, but I know he's following orders. I know he's not going to hurt me. He can't.

But I don't realize the most important thing until it's too late.

And he knows the moment I understand this. Sees his victory the instant he grabs the girl who shared her water with me. He forces her onto her hands and knees and unzips his pants.

"No!" I try to lunge at him with my arms bound behind me.

"Lou!" he calls to one of the men who appears instantly. "Make her watch."

The man, Lou, is on me in an instant, kneeling behind me. He's clutching my face in a vise-like grip and forcing me to look at Marcus, at the poor girl.

Marcus wipes the spit off his face, looks down at the girl on her knees. He splays her open and smears my spit onto her back hole.

"No, Marcus, please don't," I try. "She didn't do anything to you."

"That'll be all the lube she gets," he says as he takes his dick out. "All thanks to you."

I've seen Marcus fuck women before. I know what he's capable of. He liked me to watch. Any time my brothers wouldn't let him fuck me, he made me watch him fuck someone else. It wasn't to make me jealous. It was to torment me. Because he made sure to punish each and every one of them in my place.

"Please Marcus. I'm sorry. I—"

The girl cries out as he thrusts into her without any restraint. "Tight little asshole. She isn't going to enjoy this even a little bit," he says. Looking down to spread her wider, he thrusts the rest of himself into her.

The girl screams.

I can't look at her. "I'm sorry! God. No. Marcus, please stop! I'm so sorry!"

"Lou. Do you have a fucking concussion?"

The man behind me hardens his grip on my face. I close my eyes.

"No. Eyes open, Cartel whore. You close your eyes and I'll slit her fucking throat."

I open them. Marcus always knew exactly how to hurt me.

"Yeah, like that. Watch. And know when it's your turn, I will tear you in fucking two. You may be valuable now but that'll change. The minute it does, you're mine."

Behind me I feel Lou's erection. He's rubbing it against me through his pants and I'm going to be sick.

But I'm lucky compared to the others.

As the boat rocks, lifted high by the waves and dropped back down hard, the men stagger away, sated, for now. All but Marcus who takes his time. Who, by the time he's finished, has the girl pinned flat to the mattress, her eyes gone glassy, blood on her bottom and thighs.

"I'm going to kill you," I tell him when he finally pulls out and stands, zipping his jeans up.

"I don't think so," he says. "Stand her up," he tells Lou.

Lou hauls me to my feet and Marcus looks me over. I don't want to show him that I'm afraid, but I am.

He looks at my belly, at the dark bruise forming there.

"Can't touch your face," he says to me. "And someone's already got at you. Was it Jacob? He always did have a hard-on for you."

"Fuck you, Marcus."

"No, Scarlett. Fuck you." He pulls his belt through its loops, doubles it over, and begins.

3

CRISTIANO

Soldiers have already sealed off the dock. Dante got here and took care of it before we arrived. He went to Milan on business after the wedding, which is less than a two-hour drive from here.

He's on the docks talking to an old man. When he sees me, he gives a nod of greeting.

"Christ," my uncle mutters.

"You don't have to be here," I tell him, surveying the scene.

"I'm staying."

I walk over the gravel road, to the two bodies lying on the ground. I get to the girl first. Crouching down, I touch two fingers to the pulse at her neck, although I don't need to. She's dead. I can see it in her still open, vacant eyes.

Her arms are drenched in dried blood. She was

hugging herself. Beneath my shoes, it's seeped into the ground.

A single gunshot to the belly. It's a terrible way to die.

Straightening, I look out over the boats bobbing in the water. It's a windy day, the water rough.

The man talking to Dante points to a slip where a boat is missing. Dante nods, takes his wallet out of his pocket. He pulls out some bills and folds them over. He places them into the man's hand who looks around before taking the money.

I turn and walk across the lot to Jacob's body lying on the ground. Gunshot to the head. They weren't messing around. He probably died instantly. I feel his pockets searching for his phone. I find it in his breast pocket. It's password protected, which I knew it would be. Charlie can take care of that though. I tuck it away for later.

On the ground I find a discarded zip tie. Bending, I pick it up. It's been cut but I can't help but wonder if it had bound Scarlett. If she stood here and watched her uncle murdered. One more murder committed before her eyes.

"Cristiano," Dante calls out.

I turn to watch him as he closes the last bit of space between us, only sparing Jacob a careless glance down. Jacob's death is not a loss.

"Thanks for coming out so quickly," I tell him. I

know how he feels about Scarlett. He's doing this for me.

"They take what belongs to you, they take from me. We're family, brother. Family first, like Dad said."

I put a hand on his shoulder. "Thank you." I gesture to the old man. "Find anything out?"

"Boat that stood there was the Laura Lee. Retired fishing boat the owner has rented out to an anonymous party a half-dozen times."

"What's the capacity?"

"Will carry about twenty, twenty-four people."

"And the anonymous party?" I ask, watching the old man who'd been talking to Dante watch us. As soon as he sees my eyes on him, he lowers his and walks quickly away.

"Mexicans." He holds up a battered old phone I know isn't his. "But he's got a GPS tracker on it."

I peer at the screen, watch the little red dot in the middle of the ocean.

"Pick up the girl," I tell two of my men. We can try to figure out who she was at least. "We'll dump De La Cruz in the ocean. Let the fish get at him. Let's go get my wife."

4

SCARLETT

Darkness has fallen and it's quiet. The engine stopped about an hour ago and we're bobbing on the water. I don't know why we've stopped. I heard some of the men on the deck cursing but it's fairly quiet now.

I glance to the girl beside me. She finally fell asleep. I manage to get the jacket off my back and cover her at least a little. Not that it'll be much help against the chill or what just happened to her. You can't warm up the cold inside you after something like that. I know.

I lean back and stare up at the ceiling.

A few years ago, I came upon Diego, Angel and Marcus talking to men I'd never seen before—men who looked a lot like those who'd entered this room earlier today. There'd been three of them in the large, unused garage on the property—one of

Marcus's father's properties. More of a small warehouse than a garage for cars.

In addition to the men, there were six women. When I'd first seen them, I'd hidden and looked in from one of the broken windows. I guess some part of me knew to keep quiet.

The women were naked apart from shoes. Which strikes me as strange now considering none of us have shoes on, but most are at least somewhat clothed.

These women stood lined up against the wall, hands bound and hooked on chains hanging from the ceiling. I remember thinking that's how to hang an animal's carcass. They had on makeup that made them look almost cartoon-like in its application. They were all standing on tiptoe, even though each wore very high heels. And though none were crying, they all looked like they'd been crying for days.

My brothers were taking photographs of the women and discussing them like they were pieces of meat. Discussing how much each could bring in.

I'd moved then, stepping on a branch or dead leaves. It wasn't a loud sound, but it happened the instant they'd all stopped talking. Before I could even try to run or hide, someone grabbed me and dragged me inside that terrible place.

I remember feeling confused when I first saw my brother's faces. They wore guilty expressions, like they'd been caught. Found out. I remember thinking maybe they had a little bit of humanity in them. A little bit of conscience. I was mistaken, though.

I guess I hadn't quite put it together yet, what they intended to do to the women. How they were being sold, bid on in an on-line auction in real time as we stood there. It was sick. But I wasn't sure my brothers wouldn't do the same to me.

Except, I was valuable then. Like I am now. Then, they could use me to cement their place with Marcus Rinaldi. By then Marcus had already been going around his father, he and my brothers testing the waters, I guess.

But what they did when they caught me was worse than any physical punishment they could inflict upon me.

I look over at the girl whimpering in her sleep. At least I hope she's asleep. While the events of that night years ago play in vivid color across my mind's eye.

It was Diego's idea. He had a cruelty in him even Marcus didn't come close to. He was the oldest of my brothers and I think my father leaving his mother to marry mine and Noah's was something he never let go of.

Diego asked me to choose a girl. He'd been almost casual about it. Wearing a smile I hadn't trusted in years.

I'd refused at first, telling him to punish me. Not

them. Begging him to. I wasn't sure what they'd do to the chosen girl, but I was certain it wouldn't be good.

He'd told me again to choose. That it was either one or all.

So, I chose.

Because one was better than six, wasn't it?

God. I feel sick. I wipe my face on my shoulder, but salty tears still slide down my cheeks and into my mouth.

He didn't use a gun. It would have been bad enough if he'd used a gun, but he wanted to make a more lasting impression.

I'd seen a blood bath before then. Seen the aftermath of my parents' murders. But what Diego did next, I think it's what changed me. Broke something inside me. It's knowing it was me who chose her. Who condemned her.

And he made sure I'd never get involved again.

I don't wish I could forget that night. I owe it to that girl to remember. She died because of me.

I still hear her screams some nights. Still see my brother's rage as he wielded the crowbar down on her knees, shattering them. Then moved to her elbows as she hung there, helpless and in agony. Calculated and cruel, he beat her to death while we all watched. And all along, I knew she was dying because of me.

Just like this girl was raped because of me. I guess Marcus took that page out of Diego's playbook.

I turn onto my side, wincing with pain when I do. Marcus lined the front of my body with his belt. From my chest down, he used his belt to lash every inch of me, that terrible man holding me up, shouting at Marcus when the leather caught him, too.

I didn't scream. Not once. I know it only made him angrier, but I couldn't give him that. He stole my tears though. Those I couldn't help. At least the women quieted. Although what happened to them was a hundred times worse than what he did to me. A thousand times.

Cristiano feels years away. Me in the house on the island, in that cell, and then upstairs. At his table, in his bed. Noah. Cerberus wagging his tail, so happy to see me. It's like none of that exists now.

"Who are you?" a creaky voice asks in the darkness.

I blink, look around to locate the woman speaking. I find her on the opposite end of the mattress nearest me. There are three others sleeping between us.

"Why can't they touch you?" she asks, and I hear resentment in her words.

"I..." how do I answer?

"He called you a cartel whore. I heard him. Are you with them? The Cartel?"

"No. Of course not."

"Then why didn't he touch you? You don't have the mark."

"What mark?"

She lifts the wrist of one of the sleeping girls. A younger one. She shows me the mark made by what looks to be a black sharpie. Just an X.

"What is it?"

She drops the girl's wrist. "Virgin. They get more for the virgins. Crew can't fuck the virgins but the rest of us are fair game."

"They'll sell them?"

"What did you think they'd do?"

That was a stupid question now that I think about it.

"And they'll sell *us*. All of us. Well, maybe not you."

I try to ignore the hate in her voice. I can't blame her. "When? How?"

"You tell me, Cartel girl."

"I don't know. I'm not with them." I feel like Peter denying that he knows Jesus. "Didn't you see what he did to me?"

"Show me your wrists."

"I can't." I turn a little so she can see my arms are bound even though she already knows.

She turns her face and spits. "I know there's no mark. You're one of them. You did something to the Italian but what they do to us is still worse."

I know it is. I don't say anything but lower my gaze.

"Who are you?" she asks again.

"I'm no one."

There's a sound then, an engine. Both of our gazes flick to the window where a light shines in, waking some of the others before it's gone again.

Someone hoots and the sound of men's boots on the deck grows louder. I hear muffled words. This man is loud, though. He speaks first in Spanish then English. I can tell he's talking to Marcus, because Marcus doesn't speak Spanish. He didn't pick up a single word in all the years he worked with my brothers. Refused to because he's an arrogant fuck.

"Just fucking found it. I'm going to kill that old man," he says, and he sounds pissed.

"Get the girls," another man says as our door opens.

The women who were somehow still sleeping are startled awake now. There's an audible gasp as men enter the room.

"Let's go," the big one says, grabbing the arm of the woman closest to him and hauling her roughly to her feet.

Other men follow him in. The women don't move fast enough apparently because most have to be dragged out. I don't see Marcus at first, but I can hear him outside still talking to the other man in English.

The girl beside me lets the jacket slip as she stands. Guilt twists my belly when she meets my eyes only momentarily. I can't tell if the look is embarrassed or accusing. I have no words to comfort her either way, so I remain silent.

I'm trying to stand but the boat is rocking with all the movement. Between the rocking, the pain of Marcus's punishment, and my arms bound behind me, I can't get up without help.

Lou leers at me when he comes to haul me up. I can see he's hard again. I wonder if it's the memory of Marcus's assault on the girl or my beating that's got him aroused.

"Get off me!" I twist free as soon as I'm up. When he tries to grab me again, I smash my head into his nose. I know he'll hurt me for it, but I can't not fight. I can't let him take me and all these women like this.

"Fucking whore," he says, his grip still too tight even as he's dazed.

"Let's go," Marcus yells. When he sees it's only us in the room, he stops. "Is she giving you trouble, Lou?"

"I think the fucking bitch broke my nose."

"Not the first time it's been broken from the look of you," I say. It is bleeding but I don't think it's actually broken. Too bad.

Lou turns, raising his arm to strike.

"Whoa," Marcus catches his wrist, eyes locked on

mine. "I got her," he says. "Go make sure the others don't give our men any trouble."

"Fine."

Marcus keeps hold of me as Lou walks out of the room.

"You know, sea is pretty rough. Could be you hit your head against the wall in transport," he says, taking me by the back of my hair and rushing me toward the wall.

He smashes my head against the metal wall of the room and for a moment, I see stars. But he tugs me upright again, my ears still ringing.

"Or maybe you fall fucking overboard," he threatens as he walks me to the door.

"He'll kill you," I warn but I don't know who he is or if he would.

Marcus stops just outside and turns to me. "Maybe it'll be worth it."

I see the lights in the distance before he does. I don't hear anything though because the screams of women as they're forced from one boat to another as the rocky sea looms beneath them, muffles the sound of its approach.

But Marcus sees my face and turns to look in the same direction.

"Fuck!"

He shifts his grip to my arm and drags me across the deck toward the other boat. We're running but it's slippery and I'm resisting as much as I can.

He doesn't seem to care though. If he has to drag my body along the deck of the boat, he will, and I know it.

The fast-approaching boat shines a huge light on us. We stop and I squint my eyes against the light. I see the glint of metal in Marcus's hand as he raises his arm to shield his eyes.

"Marcus! Let's fucking go!" someone calls out from the other boat as our boat rocks with the weight of men coming on board. I can't see who they are for the spotlight, but I hear them speaking Italian.

"Rinaldi!" comes Cristiano's thunderous voice and for a moment, it's like time stops. Like we're frozen in time as he comes into view. The light too bright behind him, showing only his outline. Making him look like a giant. An angel. A god.

"Fucking boyfriend is stupid as fuck," Marcus says calmly to me.

My relief is short-lived. I know I'm not rescued just yet.

Not when Marcus presses the pistol to my temple.

5

CRISTIANO

"Not who you expected to see?" Marcus Rinaldi asks but the words don't make sense.

The crew found the tracker not fifteen minutes ago. I know because the signal went dead, but we followed the dimly bobbing light in the distance.

It's the first time I've seen Marcus Rinaldi in person since the night he murdered my family.

He's older now. A little softer around the middle, a little more worn, but by no means not a threat.

Especially not when he has Scarlett by the arm, the gun in his hand digging into her temple.

I can't look at her though. Can't think about how bruised she looks. How naked and vulnerable.

I need to keep my eyes on him.

"Drop your weapon or I kill her."

"I have no intention of shooting you. I plan on

using my hands," I say, setting the pistol down.

"No, not good enough. Into the water."

"Take the gun off her."

"I don't think so." He cocks the gun instead.

Dante comes into view in my periphery. Marcus's eyes shift to him.

"Both of you. Pistols in the water."

"Mother fucking—"

"Dante!" I order.

"I won't let him—"

"Drop it." I pick up my gun and throw it overboard. It barely makes a sound.

"Cris—"

I glance at him. "He has Scarlett."

Dante's gaze shifts from me to Marcus and back. He drops the gun into the water.

"Good boys."

I take a step toward him. I wasn't sure what I'd feel when I saw him again. Wasn't sure if all the rage over the years would burn me up, take over, turn me into a beast that's just caught his prey.

It doesn't though. And I don't know if it's Scarlett at gunpoint that has muted that beast. That's at least tempered it for now.

I take another step and hear someone from the other boat call out to Marcus. Tell him they need to move.

"You're going to miss your ride," I tell him as the boat teeters beneath us and the larger one waiting on him moves slightly farther out. "Let her go. You're not taking her with you."

"I've had my fill of her already," he says, expression cocky, his words making my hands fist.

I force myself to breathe and take another step. He's lying. It's what he does.

He backs up a step to match mine but he's out of room.

"Marcus. Let's go!" a man yells from the other boat.

Marcus turns around, drags Scarlett a step.

I charge him. I'm almost to him, only an arm's reach away. I know I can grab him. I know it.

But he does something I don't expect.

He raises an arm to shoot his pistol into the air. Scarlett screams, and a moment later, he shoves her hard and she goes toppling over the side of the boat.

In that split second, as her body tumbles overboard, I'm frozen in place.

I can have him. For years I've been living with one purpose. One goal. To kill Marcus Rinaldi.

No. Two goals.

To find out what he said to my mother and then to kill him.

But he's grinning like the fucking Joker, running to the other boat. Scarlett bobs on the water's surface just once. She can't save herself, not bound as she is, and the water swallows her scream as it swallows her body.

6

SCARLETT

It's freezing. My god. How can it be so cold?

I'm kicking but my arms are bound and I'm sinking. Just sinking. It's so dark below me. Inky black. I'm a strong swimmer and I've never been afraid of water. But tonight, I'm terrified. The open sea, the darkness of it, overwhelm me as the little bit of the light from the boats above fades too fast.

I have a few seconds, I think, before my lungs force me to breathe. Force me to take in air when all they'll get is water. Icy cold sea water.

Then I feel him. One powerful arm banding around my ribs and pulling me up with him. He's a strong swimmer too. Stronger than me. He's fully clothed and he's hauling me up with him. How did he even find me down here?

As soon as we break the surface, I open my

mouth only to suck in air and salt water. I choke on it, coughing, my nose and throat on fire.

"It's all right. I've got you," Cristiano says.

I'm not sure what's colder, the water or the air? I still can't move my arms but I'm thrashing against him, kicking wildly, desperately.

But he holds tight, keeping me above the surface. "You're safe."

Another set of hands close around my arms and I'm hauled up into the boat. A different one than the fishing boat that's bobbing, now deserted, not too far away.

I'm on my belly throwing up water. How much did I swallow in those moments I was under? It was moments, right?

Cristiano is beside me, hand on my back.

After what I hope is the last of the retching, I lay my cheek on the floor of the boat. This one doesn't stink like the other one.

I feel something cold at my back then, at my wrists. I try to pull away, but Cristiano shushes me and a moment later, my arms are free. I rub them, right hand around my left wrist first, then the other way, the skin raw.

Cristiano's hands touch my shoulders and then he's wrapping something warm around me. A blanket.

I look back at him as I hold onto the blanket. He's soaked, his eyes locked on me, watching me so closely. Dante comes into view behind him. He's soaked, too, and staring at me. Did he go in after me, too?

"Cristiano," a man says, drawing my attention.

Cristiano drags his gaze to the man.

I follow it to his uncle who looks a little worse for wear.

"We can catch up with them," his uncle says. "Get that bastard and finish this."

"No." Cristiano shifts his gaze back to me.

"What do you mean, no? He's closer than he's ever been!"

"No," his response is quiet, slow. He doesn't look away from me to answer but bends down to lift me into his arms. "Back to the island," he nods to another man. He walks us past his uncle, into an interior room and closes the door.

I realize I'm shivering. That noise is my teeth chattering.

"There's no tub," he says in that way of his, that abrupt, awkward way he has. It makes me wonder again how much he's been around people. It's not that he's uncomfortable. Not at all. He just doesn't waste words and doesn't seem to care how he comes across.

He sets me on my feet and reaches around me to run the water in the small shower. He tests it then, looks at me, takes the blanket from me.

I shudder.

He walks me into the shower and turns me to face him.

Hot water runs over me, washing the salt from my soaked hair, warming my body. It also makes the welts on my skin and my raw wrists burn. I want it though. I need the heat. I need to get what just happened off my body.

I watch him look me over and I wonder what he's thinking. He looks so pained. I guess I don't expect that.

He reaches a hand out, drenched button-down stuck to him. It's what he was wearing at the wedding, I realize. God. It feels like years have passed since then. He runs a finger over the topmost welt. I hiss in a breath and he draws back, inhaling tightly himself.

His eyes are a midnight sky when they meet mine. "What else did he do?" His voice is hoarse, tortured.

Words bubble up inside me and it's like my throat is filled with sea water again.

What else did he do?

Where do I start?

When the tears come, I drop my head. When his big hand closes around my neck to pull me into his chest, I don't resist. I don't want to. I don't have any energy left.

As strong as I've been all these years, as much as

I've fought, where has it gotten me? What has it gotten me?

People die around me.

People die because of me.

Women—girls—are violated, their lives destroyed because of me. Because of who I am. Because of my family.

My brothers may have started this, but it doesn't exempt me from blame. It doesn't exonerate me. I didn't fight hard enough because if I had, I wouldn't be standing here now. I wouldn't be wrapped up in this man's powerful arms if I'd fought hard enough. In no way do I deserve this comfort. Not when I know what's already happened to the others and what they will still endure.

All these years I've thought of my freedom. I've thought of Noah's freedom. How selfish am I? How selfish when I knew all along what they were doing, and I did nothing. Nothing apart from a ridiculous, pathetic hunger strike.

The woman who accused me of being one of them, she was right. I am.

And I am responsible.

I don't deserve to have survived tonight.

CRISTIANO

I stand with my arms folded watching from across the room as the doctor finishes examining Scarlett. She's sleeping. Didn't even fight me when I told the doctor to give her something to relax her. Something strong enough to knock her out.

"What is it about her?" Dante asks, his eyes, too, on Scarlett.

I turn to him. He shifts his gaze to mine and takes a swallow of whiskey.

"Why would you give everything up for her?" he continues.

I take a deep breath and swallow my own drink. It's not enough. "She's innocent, Dante. And she can't help her name."

He snorts.

"Why did you go in after her then?" I ask him.

"I was going after you."

"No, you weren't."

He turns his attention to pouring himself another glass, taking his time to look at me. "I'm glad she wasn't more badly hurt. Glad she didn't die. But we can't lose focus. That bastard—"

"Will be punished. I swear it on my life, Brother."

"Don't swear on your life. Don't tempt fate." He drinks.

"Fate's fucked me over too many times. It's not up to fate anymore."

"I mean it."

"I know." Guilt gnaws at me. I look at him, my younger brother who has grown as tall as me, as big, as dark. He doesn't deserve this life. "Thank you for wanting to save her."

He can't hold my gaze but nods in acknowledgement.

I smile. Because I know he'd gone in after her, not me.

"I'm going to bed," Dante says and walks out of my room.

"She wasn't violated," the doctor says a few minutes after Dante's gone. He adjusts the blanket over her shoulders and turns to me.

I exhale. Nod.

He goes into the bathroom to wash his hands then returns to the bedroom to lay out some ointments, bandages and plastic bottles of pills.

"These pain killers," I say, reading the label of one of the containers. "These are strong enough?"

"It looks worse than it is, Cristiano. She will be sore, but he only broke skin in a few places. She'll be fine in a few days." He plucks the bottle from my hand and sets it back on the nightstand. "Besides, any more would knock her out."

"I'd rather she sleeps if it's painful."

"I don't think that's up to you to decide."

I give him a look.

He ignores it and closes his medical bag. "I can stay on property if you want."

I brush a strand of hair back from her forehead. She doesn't stir. She looks younger, somehow. Softer. Her face relaxed in a way I don't often see it. I didn't want her awake, not for the examination that would tell me if Rinaldi or anyone else touched her.

With a deep exhale, I turn to the doctor. "I appreciate that, but we'll be all right." We walk out of the bedroom, where her brother and Cerberus sit anxiously outside.

Noah stands as soon as he sees us and Cerberus does the same, poking his nose at the crack in the door. He'd try to slip in if I let him. I guide him back to the hallway.

"Besides," I tell the doctor. "I'd prefer not to see you again for a good long time. No offense."

"None taken. I feel the same," he says with a

wink. I like the man. Always have. "I'll see myself out. One of your men will take me back?"

"Antonio will see to it." The doctor nods as he descends the stairs and I turn to Noah.

"How is she?" he asks, eyes wide, face that of a boy. A scared boy. She's the last of his family.

"She'll be fine. He gave her a heavy dose of a sedative, so she'll be out for a bit. Why don't you go get something to eat?" He's a bottomless pit when it comes to food.

He shakes his head, runs a hand through his hair.

"Or get some sleep. Have you slept?"

"I'm fine. It was Rinaldi?"

I nod. "And the cartel."

"Are you sure about that? Why would the cartel hurt her?"

"We'll talk to her when she wakes up and see what we can figure out."

"Can I go in there?"

"As long as you let her sleep."

"Thanks."

He moves into the bedroom and I walk to the top of the stairs. I hear the front door close and footsteps into the living room. My uncle. I walk down the stairs, Cerberus on my heels. Sending him to the kitchen, I head into the living room to find my uncle standing in front of my mother's portrait. He took a shower too, even though he didn't take a dunk, and he looks as crisp as usual. He keeps several suits on the island.

"She was a beauty," he says when I walk into the room.

"She was. I wonder if Elizabeth would have looked like her." The thought comes out of nowhere and my uncle turns to me.

"Don't go down that road. You've already lost focus."

I know why he says it. I don't like it, but I understand why. He's right. I have already lost focus. Because tonight, I had Rinaldi in my sights. Tonight, I could have taken him. I could have gotten what I needed to understand and avenge my family.

Tonight, I could have been done with it.

But I chose Scarlett instead.

And I'm not sure if it's even puzzling that I did.

I walk away, noticing the whiskey Lenore left on the coffee table and pour some into each of the tumblers. My uncle's eyes burn into my back. He's pissed.

Picking up both glasses, I turn and walk to him. I hand him one.

"You got to the old man who rented the boat?"

He nods. "He's taken care of. Not that he's any of our concern."

"He's a human being." I didn't want the cartel returning to punish the old man for the tracking device he'd had on the boat every time they'd taken it.

"Sometimes I don't recognize you, Cristiano. You even put your own brother's life at risk and for what?"

I turn to walk to the window. I feel his eyes on me as he drinks his whiskey. The sea is calmer today, the sky clearer, as the sun sets. Apart from a moonless night when stars blanket the sky, it's the most beautiful time on the island.

"What did you expect me to do? Let her die?"

He faces me, eyes hard, jaw set. "She is a means to an end. That is all. Not worth Dante's life. Or yours."

A means to an end. If I want to work with the cartel, I need her. It's why I married her. But there's something fundamentally wrong with this. Something my uncle isn't privy to. At least I don't think he is.

I don't understand myself why I did it—why I married her—because I've known all along this isn't my reason. I never had any intention of working with the cartel. I never planned for any future after killing Rinaldi.

Not that I ever contemplated suicide. Not consciously. It's more that after Rinaldi, after avenging my family's murders, the picture ends. There is only a void.

Or there was. Until Scarlett.

And whether he realizes it or not, it's what has kept me focused on the task. The thing that's kept my determination sharp.

But when the possibility of a future with Scarlett comes up, it muddies the waters. When it comes to Dante, I feel guilt at my choice. At what I've known for a long time. But with Scarlett, it's different. My guilt for Dante is to live to spare him pain. With Scarlett, it's to live. To really live.

"I wasn't going to let her die," I say finally.

The phone in my pocket buzzes and I dig it out, turning away.

Lenore enters the living room from the kitchen carrying a tray of coffee. I walk toward my study to take the call. It's Charlie.

"I've got something for you," he says.

"Am I going to like it?"

"I doubt it. You alone?"

"Yes." I close the door to my study.

"Jacob De La Cruz had a text about two hours after the wedding."

I swallow the last of my whiskey, feel the burn down my throat. "Go on."

"It's an address. You can figure out which. And one sentence."

"What's the sentence?"

"Remember what we agreed."

I grind my teeth together. "And the sender?" I'm pretty sure of his answer but I ask anyway.

"Burner phone. Untraceable."

My mind goes to Alec. To how he's injured but not dead. If the others had been killed differently, a gun fight, I'd understand how he survived. It would make more sense. But this? Him shot in the arm and the leg when everyone else took a bullet to the back of the head? It doesn't fit.

"Thank you, Charlie. You've been a great help."

"I'll keep looking, see if I can find anything else."

I disconnect the call and go to the window. From here I can see the shoreline, the rocky beach. Cerberus comes running around the corner of the house, tongue hanging out as he charges into the water. I smile when I see him. I love his innocence. It's something I lost a long time ago. But it's not only innocence that I envy. It's his freedom.

Lenore walks out behind him. She's pulling on a sweater and hugging her arms to herself as she watches Cerberus. I'm about to go back into the living room when I see my uncle walk around the corner. He's got his hands pushed into the pockets of his slacks.

It surprises me he'd go out there. First, he doesn't like the beach. Second, he isn't a fan of Cerberus and Cerberus is certainly not a fan of him.

I watch them together for a minute, but Lenore and my uncle keep their gazes on either the dog or the water. They exchange a few words, but their expressions remain the same. I don't like something about the exchange though. I don't know what it is, but it rubs me the wrong way. Maybe it's my uncle's disdain for *the help*. But he's different with Lenore, isn't he? She's more family than anything else. And even if she won't say it, I know Lenore isn't exactly my uncle's cheerleader.

Maybe I'm overthinking it.

Lenore must call to Cerberus because he emerges from the waves, shaking himself out when he's nearer my uncle. I smile. He's predictable and steadfast in his likes and dislikes.

My uncle's expression changes, and I can almost hear the curse he mutters as he wipes water off his slacks before he turns to walk back into the house.

Lenore bends to pet Cerberus, offering him a treat from the pocket of her apron before taking him back into the house.

I check my watch, doing the math to figure out what time it is in Mexico, not that I give a fuck. Pushing the button on Jacob De La Cruz's phone, I call Felix Pérez.

"Jacob," he answers on the second ring. He sounds lazy. "Is it done?" I hear him take a drag on a cigarette.

"Jacob's dead."

He clears his throat and I imagine him sobering up real quick. It takes him just a moment to get his shit back together.

"Cristiano Grigori," he says knowingly.

"It's about time we talked. You and me."

"I'd say it's past time."

"You asked if it was done when you answered the call. If what was done? Kidnapping my wife?"

"In fact, I just heard of your happy nuptials. Congratulations," he says, sounding more collected. More cocky.

"Answer. My. Question."

"I assume you got her back if you're calling. If Jacob did this, then he acted outside of my authority." I wonder if he ever gave a shit about his father-in-law. I get the feeling that answer is a no.

"What about Marcus Rinaldi. Did he act outside of your authority too?"

"Marcus is a fool. Diego and Angel made a deadly mistake working with him. I wouldn't do it. Bad for business."

"The business of selling women and girls?"

"Bad for any sort of business. He's a hothead. Unpredictable and too fucking emotional. Just take what he did to your family."

My hand tenses around the phone and I have to drag in a deep breath.

"I'm going to ask you this one more time. Did you have anything to do with my wife's kidnapping?"

"Then I'll answer you one more time. No. Why would I? What purpose would it serve for me to fuck with you? You're my potential business partner, after all."

"I'm putting you out of business, Féfé."

It goes silent for a moment and I almost have to laugh because he's bothered by it. Fucking idiot is bothered by a nickname a child gave him.

"You won't be trading in flesh in territories I control."

"Well, aren't you a man of high morals. Incorruptible. Your father's son. It got your family killed, remember."

"I will continue my arrangement with the cartel on other goods because of the other families, but this is non-negotiable. Although I have to say I'm starting to wonder if the De La Cruz Cartel isn't more trouble than it's worth. You are replaceable."

"Everyone is replaceable." He's flippant and I dislike him even more.

"I want Rinaldi's location."

"Sadly, I don't have it to give you. Did he hurt her?" he asks, and I'd almost say he is genuinely concerned. Almost.

"What do you think?"

Silence. "Will she be all right?"

"She's a fighter. Stronger than any in her family that I've met."

"I'm glad to hear that."

"I hope you are. If I learn you had a hand in this, I will kill you. Slowly."

"Then I'm in no danger." I hear him take a puff of

his cigarette. "You want an act of good will? Trust building?"

"Fuck you. You're wasting my time." I'm about to hang up when he calls out my name.

"Cristiano."

Something in his tone makes me stop.

"I will give you Rinaldi's location once I have it."

8

SCARLETT

I wake to the smell of coffee. I move, rolling onto my side, but wince and stop as soon as I do. I remember instantly why I'm sore. Everything that happened comes flooding back to me at once.

"Good morning," Cristiano says.

I open my eyes. Deep orange light, the first light of morning, filters into the room washing it in its warm glow. I watch Cristiano get to his feet from the armchair he was sitting on. His clothes look rumpled, his hair like he's been running his hands through it all night.

I'm back on the island. Back in his room. In his bed.

"Morning," I say, slow to push myself up to a seat.

"Easy." He's by my side in an instant, lifting me gently.

I suck in a breath and he draws back. Even the lightest touch hurts.

"I'm sorry," he says.

"It's okay."

He adjusts the pillows behind my back.

"Is Noah okay? Did anyone—"

"He's fine. Safe. They only hit the house you were in."

"The soldiers are dead."

He nods.

"Alec. Is he..."

There's a momentarily shadow that crosses his features but he hides it quickly. "He'll be okay. Took two bullets, but nothing fatal."

"That's good, I'm glad." I adjust the blankets, just wanting to feel their softness, their warmth. Almost not believing I'm here and safe. I look back up to find Cristiano watching me. "Did I dream your brother in the water?"

He smiles. "No. He went in after you."

"Oh. Really?"

"Really."

"How did my uncle know I was there at that house? That I was alone?"

"He was tipped off."

"By whom?"

"I don't know that yet."

I nod, look down to find I'm wearing a negligée in dusty pink. I don't remember it, but it must have been in the things Cristiano bought for me on our shopping trip. It's meant to be sexy but with my striped, bruised skin beneath it, it falls short.

"I don't remember coming back here," I say. It's true. I don't remember much after my breakdown in the shower. The thought of that makes blood rush to my face. I'm embarrassed.

That person breaking down, that woman who couldn't hold her own, that's not me. I don't lean on people. I don't trust people. Not even him. I can't.

And I'm embarrassed about it.

"You were pretty out of it," he says.

It's silent for an awkward minute and I watch him turn to the side table to pour me a cup of coffee from the small pot.

"Have you slept?" I ask.

He returns, cup in hand, eyebrows raised.

"Sleep. Did you sleep?" I repeat only to get the signature grunt as he hands me the cup. I take it. Sip the burning-hot liquid. It feels good after all that cold. The memory of the ocean, of being dumped in, sends a shiver through me. I've never been afraid of water. I don't know that I am now, but I was scared then. The vastness of it. The depth. The dark.

"Cold?" He picks up the blanket at the foot of the bed.

"I'm fine," I say, shaking my head. Clearing it. "Why did you do it?"

"Why did I do what?"

"Jump into the water after me."

"The alternative would mean you drowned," he says like he's confused by the question.

I know. I've come close to death more times than I care to remember but this one, it feels closer. More real.

"That doesn't answer my question."

He studies me, big and silent. "I wasn't going to let you drown, Scarlett."

"You could have had him."

"The cost was too high."

"I—"

"I wasn't going to let you die. Period. Is that so hard to understand?"

It is.

"Besides, I'll find him again. I'm not worried about that."

I nod and silence falls again for a long minute. I feel him close by. Feel his eyes on me. I can't look at him just yet though. "I'm not a whore." I don't know why I care if he thinks I am, but I do.

"No, you're not. I know that."

I look up at him. "Why did you accuse me of being one then?"

"I expected…" he shakes his head, gaze shifting away from me, forehead wrinkling. "No, that doesn't matter." He looks back at me. "I heard what you said. Finally."

"What did I say?"

"It won't hurt as much."

I'm surprised. I guess I don't expect to hear that. I remember the words. My words. Did I expect him to understand their meaning? Did I want him to? Why say it otherwise?

I shift my gaze away from him feeling suddenly too hot.

"Did he hurt you? Before, I mean? Did Rinaldi—"

I snap my gaze back to his. "Rinaldi didn't touch me. Not like that."

Cristiano looks confused. "Then—"

"He made me watch him hurt others, but not me," I cut him off before he can ask the question I know he wants to ask. *If not Rinaldi, then who?* That's what he wants to know.

I remember my uncle then. Shot. Dead. The bullet an utter surprise from the look on his face. I don't feel anything at the memory. Not afraid. Not upset. Not relieved.

"Do you think there's something wrong with me?" I ask.

Again, I see confusion.

"I mean I don't get upset...It doesn't bother me."

"What doesn't bother you?"

"I watched my uncle kill my brothers. I watched Marcus kill him in turn. And I can't tell you how many other murders I've seen. I don't get upset anymore. I'm not even sure I get scared. I don't feel anything when I see it. Even when I feel their blood splatter my skin, I feel nothing. Not an accelerated heartbeat. Not fear. Not upset. Nothing. I just…stand there and watch."

Grunt. He takes my coffee mug and sets it down.

I wipe a lone tear, looking down as I process. "Maybe I'm more like them than I think." *A monster.*

"They were bad men, Scarlett. I know monsters and you are not one. Not even close."

"I'm not so sure, Cristiano."

"Listen, you have many, many things wrong with you, but this isn't one of them."

His comment catches me off guard and when I look up at him, I see a corner of his mouth twitch and his eyes are bright. Opposite how dark they were on the boat. He winks and his smile stretches wide.

"Jerk."

He shrugs as if saying 'if the shoe fits'. I push the blanket off and it takes me a good minute to process the pain as I swing my legs too quickly off the bed.

"What are you doing? You need to stay in bed."

"I need to pee."

From the expression on his face, he's surprised I'd have this human need, but then he nods. Looking like he's on a mission, he puts his coffee cup down and bends toward me. He slides his arms underneath me to lift me up.

"Whoa." I hold up a hand. "I draw the line at you taking me to the bathroom."

"You could fall."

"I'll be fine. It's literally two steps away."

"Marcus did that? Put those marks on you?"

"It's nothing. I'm fine."

"But it was him?"

I nod.

"I'll punish him for it," he says after a long moment.

I give him a weak smile and he steps aside, giving me some space.

I put my hand on the nightstand, just in case, before getting to my feet and making my way to the bathroom. I'm slow, each step painful, but nothing I can't handle. When I get to the bathroom and close the door, the first thing I do is look at my reflection. I want to see how bad it is. And it's bad. There are a couple of bruises on my face but most of the damage is down my front. The marks of Marcus's belt. My wrists are raw, too, but I remind myself that it's nothing compared to what could be happening to the other women right now.

I need to talk to Cristiano about that. Need to figure out a way to help them.

After using the bathroom and washing my hands, I return to the bedroom where Cristiano is texting someone. He tucks the phone into his pocket when he sees me.

"I want to get dressed. See Noah."

"You should stay in bed. Clothes aren't going to feel good on your skin."

I shake my head, walk toward the closet.

"This is what I mean about your faults. For starters, you're stubborn as a mule," he mutters, taking my arm, his touch light.

"You mean as stubborn as you?"

"Get back in bed. I'll get you something."

"I'm fine."

"You're far from fine." He comes to stand a few inches from me. "Get back in bed. Don't make me put you there."

I raise my eyebrows, fold my arms across my chest. "You'd *put me there*?"

"And I'd tie you down if I needed to."

"I'm not even…How exactly would you put me there? I'm not a thing."

"You're really asking me that?" he asks as I realize how stupid a question it is. Without a moment's hesitation, he lifts me in his arms and carries me back to the bed. "Like this," he says as he sets me down. "Are you going to stay put or do you want me to demonstrate how I'd tie you down?"

"You're a Neanderthal."

"This Neanderthal saved your life." He points to himself then to me for the next part. "Keep your ass in bed." He turns to walk to the closet.

I sit there to watch him. Before I can decide to do

anything, he's back with a lightweight dress that he sets beside me.

"Arms up," he says.

"I can dress myself."

"Arms up, Scarlett."

I open my mouth, but he doesn't let me get a word in.

"I've seen you naked. Multiple times. Arms up."

I sigh, raise my arms high.

He lifts the negligée over my head and tosses it aside.

I band one arm over my breasts, the other casually across my lap to hide how naked I am.

His expression darkens when he looks at me, focusing on the fist print at the center of my stomach before moving over the rest of me.

"I'm sorry," he says, eyes back on those darkest bruises. "I'm sorry I left you alone. Left you vulnerable."

"You saved my life. I know what you gave up in order to do that."

He sighs, softly grasps my wrists to put my arms at my sides, then reaches into his pocket to retrieve the rings. He has both the engagement ring and the wedding band.

Lifting my left hand, he slides each one on slowly, differently than he did at the wedding ceremony. I realize he's still wearing his. Did he ever take it off?

"I promise to protect you, Scarlett." It's as if he's making the vow now.

His hands feel warm, safe. I look up to find his eyes locked on me, the look intense, carnal.

I lick my lips as one of his hands slides to the back of my head. He draws me to him, our eyes open as our lips lock. The kiss, like his eyes, deep and intense. Like him. Like he's laying claim. Possessing.

I moan, I can't help it. This feels different than the other night. *He* feels different.

With his chest against mine, he pushes me back until I'm resting on my elbows. He draws back to look at me, eyes heated, face hot. He pulls his sweater over his head and is kissing me again, my back pressed into the bed now, his body touching mine, careful to keep his weight off me.

He draws back again, hand sliding down my thigh. I hear the jangle of his belt buckle, then the sliding of his zipper.

"Scarlett?" he asks me, one hand firm around my hip.

I look into his eyes. Meet his dark, intense gaze. My heart is racing, my lips swollen, my sex wanting.

"Tell me now if you want me to stop."

I swallow, every nerve ending alive as he shifts his grip to bend my knee, pushing my leg wide. It hurts but I'm hungry for him. I want it. I want him.

"Say it. Say it now."

He's at my entrance, him hard, me wet, the skin of his cock soft and warm.

I nod, I can't speak. And when he kisses me again, I close my eyes and wind my fingers into the hair at the back of his head. Inhaling his scent, feeling his power, I'm overwhelmed by him as he slides inside me.

"Fuck." It's a grunt. He's not kissing me now, but our lips are locked. I open my eyes to watch him, see his struggle as he takes my lower lip between his teeth and moves inside me, and I know he's holding back. But I want him. I want all of him.

"Hard," I manage against his lips. "Do it hard." I need it. I need it to know I'm his. Because I want that. God. I don't understand it, but I want to be his.

"Scarlett. Fuck!"

He gives over to it then and I'm not sure it's a conscious choice. He's rough, every move of his body agony and ecstasy at once for mine. This is Cristiano. This is him raw. Naked.

His thrusts are deep and hard and measured. He draws back to look at me, to watch me, his eyes almost black now.

"I'm going to come," I say on a cry, a breath. But before the words are out, I'm coming. Coming around him, coming harder when I feel him throb, when I feel the first release, when I know he's coming, too, coming inside me. Filling me up. And I cling to him, nails breaking skin, knowing he can take it. Knowing I'm safe with him.

Something has shifted. A metamorphosis has taken place.

And I know we're not the same people we were just days ago. Not when it comes to each other. We're different. This thing between us, it's different.

CRISTIANO

I draw back looking down at her. Sweat trickles down my forehead and falls onto her cheek. She's spent, eyes dazed, mouth slack.

But I'm not finished yet.

Taking hold of both her thighs, I straighten, stand to push her legs wide.

"Cristiano—" she starts, up on her elbows.

I shift my gaze from between her legs, to her eyes, then back. The room smells of sex. Smells of us.

And I'm a man starved.

I bend my neck, lean down to her.

She gasps when I lay the flat of my tongue on her, tasting us together, tasting her. I lick from hole to hole then close my mouth over her hard little nub and suck. All at once, I hear her whimper, feel her fingers pull my hair and her legs quake in my grip. I keep her wide open and suck harder until she comes again. Her body bucks as she cries out my name over and over, breathless and panting.

Only when she's still, do I release her.

Only when she's still, do I bring my lips to hers and kiss her again, let her taste us together.

Because tonight is our true wedding night.

Tonight, is when I claim my bride. My wife.

And tonight, I vow that if any man should touch her, hurt her, fucking look at her wrong, I will kill them. I will tear them apart limb from limb with my bare hands.

10

SCARLETT

I'm exhausted. When he lifts me, I don't fight him. I have no energy left. He carries me into the bathroom, to the shower, where he sets me on the bench. He strips off his clothes and switches on the water. He tests it before turning to me, lifting me again.

"Does it hurt?" he asks.

Which part? My sex feels raw, but I like that part. The welts, yes, they sting in the hot water, but I want the heat. I still feel the cold of the ocean at my core.

I shake my head. "It's okay." I notice his stiches, wonder about his shoulder. "I never asked you how you found me," I say as he shampoos my hair, standing close enough that we're touching at all times. I like it. Like him taking care of me like this. I'll allow it for now. Just right now.

"The man who rented the boat to them had a

GPS tracker installed on it. Probably to be sure the boat wasn't stolen. They found it this time, which is probably why they were changing boats. But I knew where they were headed from previous trips. I don't know if they'll still use the location but it's a start. I have men on their way now to investigate."

"They ra...hurt some of the women in front of me," I say, unable to say the word, hating the word. "Just used them like they weren't human and then threw them aside, like you'd discard a used-up thing." I see the face of the girl Marcus chose to punish because of me. I see her pain. I don't push it away. I owe her that much.

Cristiano's jaw tightens. He switches off the water and reaches out to grab a towel. He wraps it around me before grabbing one to tie around his hips.

"Did you see anyone else at the docks?"

"Marcus and my uncle seemed to be in charge. Well, Marcus at least. My uncle worked for him, as much as he wanted to believe he ran the Cartel side of things. Not that it matters anymore. He's dead."

"It still matters."

"There was someone in the car with Marcus, but I never saw his face." I look away for a moment, thinking. Trying to remember. "It's fuzzy but I think it was him who put his jacket on my shoulders. No one else was wearing a jacket at least that I remember. Apart from my uncle and Marcus, the rest of the men looked like thugs." I look back up at Cristiano. "I was naked. He took me from the bath."

His eyes narrow infinitesimally.

"You don't remember if Felix was there?"

"I don't think he was. I'd recognize him."

He nods.

I squeeze the water from my hair as I step out of the shower.

"How many women were there?" he asks.

"Maybe a dozen. They killed one on the docks. She tried to run and one of the men shot her in the stomach."

"We found her. I took her to a local morgue. We may be able to identify her. Try to find her family at least.'"

"What about my uncle's body."

"Fish food."

"Good."

I follow him into the bedroom and watch as he steps into briefs and a pair of jeans before turning to take the towel from me. I stand naked as he slips the dress over my head. It's thin, more for summer than now, but at least it doesn't irritate my skin.

"They were pretty young, some of them."

"Perverts like them young."

"I know."

He pauses as he slips his arm into a black button down and studies me for a beat too long.

I clear my throat and glance away. "One of the women said they'll be sold."

"That's right."

"And that virgins bring in more money. They'd marked them so the crew wouldn't touch them."

Although I see irritation on his face, he doesn't reply.

"Can we find them? Stop them from selling these women?"

He breathes in deeply and takes hold of my shoulders. "*You* will concentrate on healing. *I* will take care of what needs to be taken care of."

"What does that mean?"

"That means you'll stay on the island, in the house, and out of harm's way."

"No. I'm helping those women. What happened to them is partially my fault."

He looks at me with utter disbelief now. "I'm going to guess math wasn't your strongest subject."

"What does that have to do with anything?"

"How do you get to this being remotely your fault?"

"My brothers started this. My brothers and Marcus did this. I don't even know how many people they've hurt."

"Your brothers. Marcus. Not you." He picks up one of the containers the doctor left, reads the label and pops the lid. Two pills drop onto his palm. "Here."

"What are those?"

"Painkillers."

"I'm fine."

"You're not fine. I see that it hurts. Take them."

"I said I'm fine."

"You punishing yourself won't help them."

"I said no. Remember when you didn't want anything when the doctor reset your shoulder? I don't want anything now and I'm pretty sure that hurt more than this."

"Christ," he mutters, dropping the pills back into the bottle and securing the lid. "Like I said, stubborn as a mule." He walks to the door and opens it.

"Like I said, as stubborn as you." I walk out into the hallway. "I want to help them, Cristiano. I mean it."

"You leave that to me."

"Scarlett!" Noah appears at the bottom of the stairs and it takes all I have not to charge down toward him. Well, all I have and Cristiano's hand around my wrist.

"Easy, she's hurt," Cristiano tells him once we're downstairs and I go in for a hug.

Noah nods and tries to hug, but not hug me, all at once.

"You can hug me. I want you to hug me," I tell him.

"You hurt her, and we have a problem," Cristiano growls beside me.

"Don't listen to him," I say, but this other side of Cristiano, this predator turned protector is strange. Unexpected. He's a beast but he's got a soft side. I like when it comes through.

Noah squeezes me hard and it does hurt but I don't care. In his hug I feel how young he is, how much he's lost and how much he needs me, even if he tries to act like a man.

"Aren't you late for your lesson," Cristiano asks him, checking his watch.

"What lesson?" I ask, looking at him.

Noah, looking guilty, shifts his gaze to Cristiano.

"Self-defense," Cristiano answers after a beat.

I narrow my eyes. "You're teaching him how to fight?"

"Not me personally."

"Noah's not some street fighter. He's not a thug."

"Sis—"

"He needs to learn how to protect himself, protect his family," Cristiano says.

"And how would fighting help in a gun battle? Because all the fights I've seen so far involve enough gun fire to call it a war." It dawns on me then what exactly the lesson is. "You're teaching him how to use a gun?"

"He should already have been taught."

"No. I told you, I don't want this for him."

"And I told you it's been decided."

Noah slips away quietly as Cristiano takes my

shoulders and walks me backward to the wall. Out of earshot of anyone.

"Whether or not you chose this life, it chose you. You're in it. So is your brother. Period. We have enemies, Scarlett. And right now, you and your brother are among the very few I can trust. The boy needs to learn how to shoot. For his own protection and for yours."

"He's fifteen."

"Did you understand what I meant when I told you that Jacob was tipped off?"

I stare up at him, feeling the line form between my brows.

"Think. Who knew where you were?"

"Anyone in your organization could know."

He shakes his head. "Only a handful of people knew of the existence of that house to begin with. Even my own uncle didn't know where we were."

"So, you think it was the soldiers? They're all dead. I think that clears them."

He raises his eyebrows like he's telling me to think harder.

"Alec?" I whisper but I don't believe it. "He's more than loyal to you. He loves you. I saw how he was when you were hurt. He didn't betray you, Cristiano. He wouldn't."

"Us. Betray us."

"It wasn't him. I'd stake my life on it."

"I wouldn't."

Someone clears their throat. I look over Cristiano's shoulder and see his uncle, David.

Cristiano releases me and turns to him.

"You're all right?" he asks me.

I nod but my brain is whirling, trying to make sense of what Cristiano just said. Of what he thinks.

"I'm glad." David replies but I wonder if he truly is. I haven't forgotten what he did when I walked into his house.

Just then I hear a bark and a moment later Cerberus turns the corner, Lenore on his heels.

"That dog is as stubborn as his master," Lenore tries to complain but I hear how much she loves both the dog and his master.

Cristiano catches Cerberus before he can jump on me.

"Easy, boy."

Lenore looks me over and smiles. "You look better than I'd expected. I'm glad you're safe, Scarlett."

I don't mention the welts and bruises beneath the dress, but bite back the pain as I bend down to cuddle Cerberus instead. Her gaze momentarily flicks to my hand, to the rings on my finger. I'm not sure if I see disappointment briefly on her face or if I imagine it. I'm not looking directly at her but when I do, she smiles almost proudly at Cerberus or me.

"I'm going to go get some rest after last night,"

David says. "I wanted to see for myself you were all right before I left," he says to me.

"Oh, thanks."

I see Cristiano's expression of surprise before he masks it. "I'll walk you out, Uncle."

"I hope you're hungry for breakfast. Cristiano made sure I made anything you could possibly want to eat."

I chuckle. "I am hungry." I follow her into the dining room, Cerberus padding along at my side.

11

CRISTIANO

I watch her through the day. Hell, I watch everyone. I still have one question for her that I can't make sense of myself. Well, more than one, but this she'll need to answer tonight.

"Walk with me," I tell her after dinner. It's a clear night, the moonlight silvery on the calm water.

She was in that water, I think. In the dead of night in the pitch-black sea. I wonder if she thinks about it, too. It was sheer determination that I found her in there. If I'd waited another second, she'd have been lost. Bound as she was, she went straight down.

I help her into her coat and button it up. Cerberus is already at the door waiting for his nighttime walk. I've been doing this with him for as long as I've had him. Only the location has changed.

Cerberus leads the way, charging toward the sea without a care.

"Be careful," I tell Scarlett, hand on her arm to steady her when she trips almost as soon as she's outside.

"Do you like being here on your own? I mean on the island so far from people," she asks.

"I don't like people. In case you haven't noticed."

"Oh, I noticed."

"And I'm not alone. Lenore is here. I have soldiers and—"

"Soldiers don't count."

"Then Lenore is here. And Cerberus. I need to ask you a question, Scarlett."

I see her turn to me in my periphery and take my eyes off Cerberus to face her.

"Okay." She must sense the seriousness of it because she seems to brace herself.

"He didn't touch you. The doctor checked."

"What?"

"Marcus didn't violate you."

Her eyebrows nearly disappear into her hairline. "You had the doctor check?"

I nod.

"While I was unconscious? Without my consent?"

I wait for her to process because yes, of course I did. Who wouldn't have done that?

"In what world do you think that's okay to do?" she asks.

"My world." I answer simply and honestly.

"Of course. You would. Why am I surprised?" She shakes her head, grits her teeth. "Why didn't you just ask me if he touched me? Did that even occur to you?"

"I wanted to be sure."

"What did you think? I'd lie to you?"

"You might. You might feel embarrassed."

"You should have asked me. *You* violated me by doing such a thing without my permission." She spins to walk away but I catch her by the arm.

"You're my wife. I have a right to know."

"I'm your wife in name only."

I feel my eyebrows arch. "I don't think so. I thought I made that clear this morning, *Little Kitten*."

"Back to that again?"

"You prefer Fury?"

"I prefer my name. Scarlett. Just Scarlett."

I smile, wrap my hand around the back of her neck and pull her to me. Leaning closer, I bring my face to hers and inhale her scent. My soap. My shampoo. I like it on her.

"I can still taste you on my tongue, *Scarlett*," I say, my voice low and deep in the quiet night.

Her eyes go wide, and I can't help but laugh. She shoves at my chest, but I don't let her go.

"You're my wife. Period."

She stops pushing. "You said you'd let me go when this is done. You'd let Noah go."

I did. I remember. "It's not over yet, is it? To bring it up is premature."

"Does that mean you still will?"

I study her. Cerberus barks once, coming toward us with a stick he's found washed up on the shore. Grateful for the interruption, I bend to take it from him and toss it for him to retrieve before turning back to Scarlett.

She looks pretty in the moonlight. I like that she doesn't wear makeup. She's just herself.

When she turns to find me watching her, she folds her arms across her chest and opens her mouth. I speak before she can.

"I haven't asked you my question yet," I say.

She shakes her head. "I'm all ears."

"*Why* didn't he touch you? He had the opportunity. I saw his face on the boat, not that I'd need proof to know, he hates you as much as he hates me. Maybe more. It makes no sense that he didn't touch you."

Her forehead wrinkles and she rubs it, then meets my eyes. "He wasn't *allowed* to."

"Ah."

She raises her eyebrows.

"I spoke with Felix Pérez today."

"Felix?"

I nod.

"Do you really think he's taken over the cartel? I'm telling you, Cristiano, he wasn't capable."

She's wrong on that.

"What did he say?" she asks.

"He claimed not to know about Jacob's death. Although he didn't seem all that bothered by it. And he swore he had nothing to do with your kidnapping."

"But you don't believe him?"

"No. And I still don't have one piece of the puzzle."

"Who gave up the location of the house."

I nod.

Scarlett's forehead wrinkles. "From what I remember, Felix was never that clever."

I give her a one-sided grin, wrap my arm around her waist and turn her. "The ones you don't think twice about, who fly under the radar, they're usually the most clever, Little Kitten."

The wind picks up as if eavesdropping on our conversation. Scarlett shudders.

I shift my arm to wrap it around her shoulders and whistle for Cerberus.

"Let's go to bed, Scarlett. I want to feel you beneath me again."

12

SCARLETT

I'm trying to wrap my brain around Felix Pérez taking over the cartel. Maybe I don't remember him correctly. I was pretty young, I guess. I just can't imagine it. He was more like an annoying bug that keeps buzzing by your ear. I remember neither of my parents liked him. But I'm not sure they liked Jacob either. I know my mom didn't. She didn't trust him, and my dad didn't trust anyone who wasn't blood. Even though Jacob took on the De La Cruz name, he was and always would be an outsider. And Felix marrying Jacob's daughter, his niece, meant nothing to my father.

I think about that. About only trusting your own blood. That got my father killed. Blood is overrated.

"Cristiano," I start once we're upstairs. "Are you sure about Felix?"

He closes the door behind us. "I'm sure of one

thing at the moment," he says, unbuttoning my coat and slipping it off. He does the same with his and tosses them over the back of a chair. He spins me so my back is to him and unzips my dress. "I don't want to talk about Felix or the cartel or any of it just for a little while." He turns me to face him and slips the dress off my shoulders. It's loose enough that it slides right off. I'm naked underneath. "Right now, all I want to do is look at my beautiful wife."

His gaze slides over me, fist tightening as he takes in the striped flesh before drawing in a slow, deep inhale of breath. He closes his eyes momentarily, but when he opens them and looks at me, that anger is checked. Not gone, just cataloged for later.

"Right now, all I want to do is show my wife exactly how much she is mine."

I don't resist when he kisses me then. I don't want to. My body remembers earlier. It remembers how he felt on top of me. Inside me.

Arms wrapped around me Cristiano walks me back to the bed. He sits me on the edge and pushes me backward so I'm lying flat, legs dangling off.

"Open them." He gestures to my legs.

I swallow, take in the darkness of his eyes.

"I said open them, Scarlett."

I do. I spread my legs and watch his eyes dip down to my sex.

"Wider."

I lift my feet onto the bed and feel my face heat up as I expose myself to him.

As he unbuttons his shirt, he drags his gaze from my sex to my eyes. "Touch yourself," he says, pulling the shirt off, then moving to pour himself a whiskey. He takes a seat on the armchair directly across from the bed. "Show me how you make yourself come," he says, taking a sip and reclining back, long legs spread wide as he watches me, elbow on the armrest, head resting against the chair's back.

"I...I don't think I can do that," I stammer, feeling embarrassed.

He grins. "I think you can. I'm pretty sure in fact. Do it. Put your fingers on your clit and rub."

I'm tentative but I reach to touch myself. I'm swollen and wet already. He watches me casually, drink in hand. Fuck, it's turning me on.

"Good girl. Now dip your fingers inside yourself and smear your juices all over. Good. Like that."

It feels good. I like watching him watch me. I see the steel bar of his erection and I like that too. It makes me feel powerful.

"That's it, sweetheart. Let me hear you. Let me hear how wet you are."

I lick my lips and press my finger inside myself.

"You can do better than that, Kitten. Another finger."

I add a second finger keeping, the heel of my hand pressing against my swollen nub.

Cristiano swallows more of his drink then sets the glass aside and unbuckles his belt. Unzips his pants. He grips himself, pushing pants and briefs down as much as he needs to, and I watch him work his cock, pumping slowly, one corner of his mouth quirked upward as he watches me watch him.

"You like watching me?" he asks.

I lick my lips and nod.

"Dirty girl," he says with a sly smile. "I like watching you too, though." To my disappointment he tucks himself back into his pants and gets to his feet. Standing between my legs, he uses a hand to push one thigh wider. "And I think you like that. You like me watching you," he says, looking down at my open pussy, my fingers working over my clit, dipping inside me.

I nod, my mouth hanging open, even though he wasn't asking it.

"Say it." He crouches down, keeping one leg wide. "Say it if you want my mouth on you." He gives a teasing flick of his tongue over my clit and I buck, pushing my hips up. "Say it."

"I like it. I like you watching me."

"Good girl." He takes the wrist of the hand working my clit and draws it away to close the whole of his mouth over the hard nub. He lays his tongue flat over my sex and licks, then sucks. I'm so close. So close to coming. But then he draws back. Puts my fingers back on me and stands.

"Why—"

"Shh. Don't come yet but don't stop playing with yourself. I want to hear all those wet sounds."

I nod, wanting to please. Wanting to come. I lick my lips. He strips off his pants and briefs so he stands naked between my legs. His thick cock ready, the head already wet. He pushes my legs wider. It's almost painful how wide and looks down at me.

I'm dripping.

He leans toward me and slides his length into me, stretching the tight passage, making me gasp. Making me want.

"You're so fucking tight," he says, drawing out, then pressing in again before slipping completely out. He puts my hand back between my legs and grips his cock.

"I want to come," I say, my voice small.

"I bet you do." He puts his free hand over mine and together we each press a finger inside me.

"Cristiano...I want..."

He draws his finger out, then in again, and my eyes close.

"Look at me," he says. "Keep looking at me."

"Good. And keep playing with your clit. Like that. Good girl."

He draws back, cock in hand, watching.

"Tell me something," he asks. "How do you think it's going to feel having my cock down your throat?" Before I've processed, he takes my arm. "On your knees, Kitten, and keep your dirty little fingers on your clit."

He slides me off the bed so I'm at eye level with his thick cock.

"Cris—"

"Shh." He takes his thumb over the head of his cock and bends to put that finger to my mouth.

"Lick."

I do and he tastes good.

"Now suck."

I do again and I watch him watching me as I create suction around his thumb.

"Harder. Good. Like that."

He straightens again and withdraws his finger.

I lick my lips.

"Are you close?"

I nod.

"Good. Open your mouth."

He pushes between my lips, his hand fisting my hair to tug my head back, as his cock hits the back of my throat.

I choke and he grins, backs off.

"I—"

But I don't get to finish. I only have time to take a quick breath before he's pushing in again, his eyes darkening as he moves faster and I'm aroused watching him, tasting him, looking up at him as he towers over me, controlling me.

A moment later, he mutters a curse and pushes

deeper still, and I feel him throb, feel his release and when I do, I come too. I come on my fingers, moaning around him, tasting him, watching him.

When it's over, when he's finally empty, he pulls slowly out and crouches down. Kissing my cheek, he holds my chin with two fingers. He looks at me and smiles.

"Swallow."

I want to, it's just so much. I nod and he brings his thumb to the corner of my mouth to wipe it clean.

"All of it," he says, and I swallow again. When I do, he kisses my mouth and I wonder if he tastes himself. I kiss him back.

A few moments later, he lifts me in his arms and lays me on the bed. And when he climbs in beside me, I turn to him, burrow into his chest, liking the feel of his arms around me. He pulls the blankets around us and I feel safe for the first time in too long to care that I'm lying in the arms of the man who should be my enemy.

13

CRISTIANO

I'm back again. On the cold marble floor lying in a pool of my own blood. Men are yelling, my brothers sobbing. My sister, I didn't even see her. They killed her in her room.

My mom...she's begging, pleading for the lives of her children. She's not even asking to be spared herself. But he doesn't care. He's laughing. I hear that too. And I open my eyes just enough to see him lying on top of her. To hear him breathe heavy while she lays still whimpering. He has the knife at her throat and this time when he says the words, he looks at me.

Is that how it happened? Or is it my imagination perverting the memory.

His mouth moves and his grin makes him look like a mad man. I hear the whisper, but not the words. Never the words.

I know this dream. This nightmare.

But then it shifts.

The chaos is gone. No guns. No screaming women. No sobbing children.

Words sound around me, making no sense. A man and a woman. An argument. Lights overhead too bright after so much dark. The smell is clinical. The room, when I glimpse it through heavy-lidded eyes, harsh white.

"It's too much...permanent damage." It's the woman's voice. She's trying to whisper but the words are hissed like she's angry.

The man's words are incomprehensible, just murmurs. He's calmer than she is. Then everything goes quiet. Almost everything. The only sound I hear is my voice.

I feel the prick of a needle. It doesn't hurt. I'm used to it.

Then another sound. Shoes on the floor, low but there. Hearing is my only sense. Well, that and smell. And I can smell a familiar scent.

I open my eyes with a sharp breath in. It takes me a minute to remember where I am. I scrub my face, looking over at Scarlett lying beside me. She's undisturbed.

My phone buzzes with a message alert. I check it and see four messages all within minutes of each other. That's what must have woken me.

I open the text window. It's Antonio telling me to

call him. I assume it's an update on the destination of the boat that held Scarlett and where it went to on its last four voyages. The other images are of some broken-down room. A shack almost. Inside are scraps of clothing, remnants of food containers. Stains on the floors and walls. More on the single rotted mattress.

Scarlet mutters something. I look down at her, see her lips move, her forehead furrow. I doubt either of us will ever sleep peacefully. We've seen too much.

"Shh," I tell her.

Her hand opens, fingertips brush my chest and she says one word. "No."

"Shh, you're safe. Safe."

As if she hears me, she quiets, her breathing leveling out.

I climb out of the bed, draw the blanket up over her shoulder and pick up a discarded pair of jeans. Pulling them and a sweater on, I walk out of the bedroom barefoot, running a hand through sleep-mussed hair.

The first part of the nightmare is the recurring one. It's the one that keeps me from sleep.

The second part though? That's new. I don't know if it's a dream or a memory. It has the feeling that memories do. There's a texture to it different than dreams.

I have a takeaway this time.

The man was my uncle. He's been wearing the same cologne for as long as I can remember. Something made especially for him. My father used to make fun of him for that.

I stop, smile. A strange, unimportant detail but a detail. A memory.

A soldier greets me downstairs. I'm keeping them both inside and outside for now. I check the time. Four in the morning.

"Good morning," I say, and continue to my study, but pause when I hear noise in the kitchen.

I glance to the soldier.

"Lenore's up," he says.

I'm surprised. It's not like her to be up in the middle of the night. I walk to the kitchen to find Lenore muttering something as she plays with the nobs of the oven.

"What are you doing awake?" I ask her.

She startles, spins to face me. "Cristiano! You scared me half to death."

"Sorry."

Cerberus walks sleepily toward me and I lay a hand on the top of his head.

"I couldn't sleep," she says.

"That makes two of us. What's going on?"

She picks up the pot of coffee and pours me a cup. "Nothing. I'm sure it's fine."

"What?"

She sits at the table. "Alec. I knew he could get

hurt but I never expected it, I guess." She takes a tissue out of her pocket and wipes her eyes and nose.

I'm unmoved. Not because I think she's ingenuine. I just have seen worse. "He's alive. He'll heal," I say.

"Is she worth it?" Lenore asks.

"Excuse me?"

She shakes her head. "Never mind. Don't listen to me."

I study her. "What were you and my uncle talking about on the beach yesterday?"

"What?"

"You took Cerberus out. He followed. I was in the study. Saw you from my window."

"Oh." She shrugs a shoulder and shifts her gaze away momentarily. "Nothing special. I was surprised he'd followed me out. He said he wanted to check in on Alec but, well, you know how I feel about that man."

"Why do you feel that way about him?"

"Ah, that's an old story and one not worth telling. Would you like some breakfast?"

"Did you ever come see me when I was in the coma, Lenore?"

"What?"

"When I was sedated." It was a medically induced coma to let my body heal. "Did you come see me?"

"Only a few times. I would have liked to come

more often, but your uncle wanted to keep your location a secret. Keep the fact that you and Dante survived a secret. And it made sense."

I nod.

"Why do you ask?"

"Nothing. Just curious." I feel a buzz in my pocket and reach in to see it's Antonio with another notification. "I need to go."

She nods. "Let me know when you're ready for breakfast.

I head to my study, Cerberus walking beside me, considering my strange conversation with Lenore. There, I dial Antonio.

"I have some news though not much."

He knows I rarely sleep, and I know he's the same as me so there's no mention of the time.

"Tell me."

"Found the man hired to meet the boat with a truck and transport the cargo, then walk away."

"And he was forthcoming with this information."

"For a fee."

"Of course." Mercenary. Most people in this business are.

"The house he took them to is a few miles inland. Actually, I don't think you could call it a house. I sent you some photos."

"I got them."

"The man took us there. It looks like they left in a hurry, whoever it was that was here. I'm guessing in the past they've held the women here before shipping them off to wherever they ship them off to."

"Find out yet who owns the property?"

"Land is owned by a local. He rented out the shack to a man with an accent who paid cash a few days prior. The landowner made sure not to be anywhere near the property for the agreed upon amount of time. Same man every time who worked out the deal and paid him.'"

"Description?"

"Tall, dark hair, foreign."

"That helps." Not. "I can't imagine it's Felix or Marcus actually doing this part, though."

"Last time they were here was a few months back, although they had rented the space but no-showed. Wherever they took their cargo this time, it wasn't here."

"Dead end, then."

"Not quite. Our friend who transported the cargo heard them mention something more than once. They referred to it as the big auction. Some of the women, mostly the younger ones, were separated for this."

"When's this big auction?" I ask, thinking about what Scarlett said about the marked girls.

"Soon, I'd guess. This was to be the last shipment before it would be held. I do have a city although I'd like to do some checking. It's not where I'd expect an auction like this to take place. I've already talked to Charlie about it, but I'll use my own contacts, too."

"I trust your instinct but where will the auction be held?"

"Rotterdam."

"Rotterdam?" That surprises me. It shouldn't though. Money is money and you can buy silence anywhere, even in highly developed Northern Europe.

"All right. Thanks Antonio. You've done well. Let me know when you know more."

"You're welcome."

14

SCARLETT

"Wake up, Scarlett."

I groan, trying to swipe away the hands shaking me.

"Come on. This is serious."

When I register that it's Noah, I blink my eyes open, rubbing them. He's in Cristiano's bedroom and he looks anxious.

"Hey," I sit up, looking at the clock. Eight in the morning. "You're up early." I pull the covers up. I'm naked underneath.

"This has been bugging me for days. I wasn't sure and I don't know, maybe I'm wrong but," he stops mid-sentence shaking his head.

"What is it?"

He holds up the small framed photo of Elizabeth Grigori and her friend that had captured his attention the day of the wedding. God. That feels like a lifetime ago.

"What are you doing with that? Did you take it from Elizabeth's room?"

He nods.

"I don't think you should go in there."

"I think I know her."

"What? That's impossible, Noah. She's dead. She's been dead for ten years."

"No, not Elizabeth. The other girl."

"The other girl?"

"I know. It sounds crazy. Do you remember when they first killed mom and dad?"

I nod. Of course, I do. I could never forget that.

"Remember they left me in Mexico at the beginning." They'd brought me to Italy right away.

"You're making me nervous."

"She was there."

I scratch my head. "That's impossible."

"I'm telling you I remember her. I don't think I could ever forget her face. Jacob had me play with her because she wouldn't stop crying. I remember staring at her and her staring back at me. We couldn't understand each other. I get it now. I didn't speak Italian and she didn't speak Spanish."

"Are you saying they brought her to Mexico?"

"Maybe? I thought her name was Lizzie. She kept saying something, but I couldn't understand. But, I mean...it was ten years ago. I was five. I just...I remember how sad she was, and I didn't understand what had happened to our parents, our family. I just knew they were gone, and you were gone, and everything was different. Then there was this little girl."

"You're sure?"

"I'm not sure but I don't know, I can't shake the feeling. They told me her name was Elizabeth, Scarlett. And the girl kept saying something about a Lizzie. I remember that because it was such a strange sound, those z's. She was only there for two weeks before she was gone."

"Gone?"

"Yeah. I don't know where or anything. I'm just thinking out loud here, but is it possible they thought they had taken Elizabeth but took her friend by mistake? I mean, I'm looking at their faces and this is the girl." He points to Mara.

"You haven't told Cristiano?"

He shakes his head. "I didn't know what to do. I mean, what if I'm wrong?"

"Do you know where they took her?"

He shakes his head.

I chew my bottom lip. "Jacob brought her?"

He nods.

"Was she ever alone with him, do you know? With Jacob?"

"I don't know," he answers, and I see confusion on his face. He sees I'm suddenly anxious. Urgent in my questioning. "Why does that matter? I mean, I guess so."

No. If she was only five, he wouldn't have done anything. If they thought she was Elizabeth...I shake my head. "Okay. Let me think. We need to tell him."

"What are you two doing?"

Both Noah and I startle, turn to find Dante standing in the doorway. He stalks inside.

"What are you up to?" he asks. "It looks like I interrupted something."

"What would we be up to?" I ask, hating that I'm in bed, hating that I'm naked. It puts me at a disadvantage.

"You tell me, Scarlett." I look at him now and it's hard to reconcile him with the man who'd jumped into that dark sea to save my life.

But his gaze fixes on the photo in Noah's hand and rage takes over. "What the hell are you doing with that?" he snags it away. For a moment, I see a shift in his expression, a tenderness in his eyes, but it's gone the moment he turns his gaze back to me.

He's the more emotional brother of the two. The more impulsive.

Noah opens his mouth, but I put my hand on his arm. "Nothing. He remembered that I had the same dress when I was little. That's all." It's a bad lie but it's all I can come up with.

He looks at me suspiciously then turns to Noah.

"I was coming in here to ask if you were okay," he

says to me. "But then I see you two whispering. Plotting."

"We're not plotting—"

"Don't go in my sister's room again," he tells Noah. "Don't touch anything of hers." He shifts his gaze back to me, a warning in his eyes. "I hope my brother won't regret choosing to save your life over avenging our family."

With that, he walks out and slams the door behind him.

"What the fuck is wrong with him?" Noah asks.

I'm jolted by the last part of Dante's comment. I'm still absorbing the shock of it. I want to tell Noah that he's just an asshole, but I see the way he is with Cristiano. I see how he just looked at the photo. And even if he did just jump into the water to save me for his brother, it's something. Can I blame him for hating me? Hating us?

"He's just trying to protect himself and his brother," I tell Noah, but I feel a sadness inside me. Because no matter what, I will always be the sister of the men who killed Cristiano's family.

15

CRISTIANO

The expression on Charlie's face is a grim one as he walks into my study.

"It's late," I say, looking at my watch although I know what time it is. He's made a point of arriving when no one else would be here. "Whiskey?"

"Yeah," he says, surprising me. He doesn't drink when doing business and there's no doubt this is business. He sets the thick envelope he brought with him on the desk, unbuttons the button of his tailor-made suit and takes a seat. "A double."

I study him as I pour a glass for him and refresh mine. Something has him ruffled. He was one of the people Dante called when he found us that morning after the massacre. I still think about that. About what it must have been like for my brother to be greeted by that horror.

He'd gone out the night before. Snuck off the island to meet a girl when he was supposed to be at home. He told me he hadn't been able to make sense of what he was seeing because he wasn't sure if it was all the alcohol. If he was still drunk. If that's why he retched so badly.

I wonder if it's the deaths themselves or finding us like we were that did the most damage. I'd bet the latter.

He doesn't talk about it. He's never talked about it.

"Is Dante around?" Charlie asks. The timing strikes me considering my thoughts.

I shake my head. "He went to bed."

"That's good." His face is grave. Charlie is Dante's godfather. He's always been good to him. To both of us. I know he worries, too, about Dante's state of mind at having been the one to find us. Sometimes I wonder what he'll do when this is over. When revenge is taken. What's next for my little brother? Is there anything? Or is he like me? Like I had been until only very recently.

"Here you go," I hand Charlie a tumbler and take my seat behind the desk.

He holds his glass up in a toast that I know isn't a happy one. Charlie's in his late forties now. His thick dark hair has a single, wide gray patch at his temple. He's had it as long as I can remember, and it makes him look distinguished.

"I'm not going to like this, am I?"

"No, you're not."

He opens the large envelope and pulls out the thick stack of papers inside. From here I can see bundles clipped together made up of photographs, sheets of paper and even some newspaper clippings.

"Don't keep me in suspense."

He smiles but it's half-hearted. He extends the pages out to me and I reluctantly take them. I only glance down quickly before shifting my gaze back to his.

I feel the tattoo I'd drunkenly carved onto my arm burn. I knew this was coming, didn't I? It's why I asked in the first place.

"Those are the names you asked me to look into."

I breathe. Try to manage the tension growing inside me.

I know what he's going to say. I've suspected it on some level. But I'm still not ready for it.

"Those people," he gestures to the stack. "They all have exactly one thing in common."

I remain silent still.

"They'd made an enemy of your uncle."

I drop the stack and get to my feet, shaking my head. "You're wrong."

Turning to the window, I look out onto the water. I wish I could be out there. Out there with her. I wish

I could hold her and listen to the waves with her and not have any of this other shit going on.

"You're wrong," I repeat, turning to face him again. Although I've never thought Charlie and David enemies, they are not friends. They never were.

"I'm not wrong and you know it. It's taken me over a year to get this together. I've been diligent, considering who he is to you."

I turn to him. "You hate him. It's no secret."

"No, that's not a secret."

"Why?"

"Look through it, Cristiano."

I pick up my whiskey and swallow the contents of the glass, feel it burn down my throat.

"Go on," he insists. "You suspected it. It's why you asked me to look into it. Look at them," he says.

"My uncle saved my life. He could have let me die."

"He's using you. He's always used you."

I slam a fist into the desk. "He saved my fucking life!"

He stands, leans over the desk to reach the pages, turns them so he can sort through them.

"I'll start at the most recent," he says, unperturbed. Charlie isn't a violent man. He's an attorney. But he's not afraid of me.

I don't look directly at the bundles as he lays

them out but the first set of names I recognize at quick glance. The latest couple.

"They were in business with David for some years, but that business came to an abrupt end when they realized he was stealing from them. Just putting a little aside every month."

"Why would he do that? He has enough money."

"He's greedy. He's always been greedy. Always had his eye on what didn't belong to him."

"What does that mean?"

He exhales, looks away like maybe he's said too much.

"Charlie. What does that mean?"

He turns back to me. Studies me. "You weren't that young. You had to have seen it."

"Seen what?"

Charlie's expression changes, emotions he is so good at keeping hidden creeping to the surface. Sadness, then anger. I recognize both.

"How he looked at your mother."

"My mother?"

He grits his teeth. I watch his struggle to maintain control. He never mentions missing her or missing the family. David does. He tells me often that he misses them. But I see it in Charlie sometimes. He hides it well, but now and again, I'll catch him looking at a photo or a painting or something of mom's especially, and it's been happening more since I came back to the house.

Charlie and my mom had a special connection from the beginning. I remember my uncle's sneer when Dante mentioned it. When he told me the story of their friendship.

Charlie and my mom were good friends from university days. And at the time in his life when he'd been coming out, she'd been a support to him. I'd never known whether my uncle's dislike of Charlie had to do with his sexual preference or his close relationship with my mother.

"No," I say. Because if I'd seen that, even if I can't remember it, wouldn't I have some sort of muscle memory, some instinct to warn me against David?

"The next man, Fred Barnaby, this one got a little uglier. He blackmailed your uncle. Or attempted to until you took care of him."

I remember Barnaby. Remember the comment he'd made asking me if *that cheat* had sent me, his thug.

"I could go on," he says. "But I think you're intelligent enough to do this yourself. It's time you opened your eyes, Cristiano. The stakes are higher now." There's a pause. "There's Scarlett to consider. Her life is in danger."

Am I so obvious to him? Who else sees right through me? Sees this vulnerability?

"She's under your protection now. As is her brother. And I know you take those things seriously."

I don't deny it. Instead, I nod, my gaze on those pages although I've unfocused my eyes so the words are a blur.

"You didn't see his face when he told me they'd taken her, Charlie."

He doesn't comment, just holds my gaze, as if to say you and I both know that's bullshit. And he's right. My uncle has a different face for every occasion. I just never thought of him using them with me.

"He didn't know Scarlett's location. It couldn't have been him who tipped off Jacob."

"Couldn't he have known? Didn't he come get you from that strip club?"

I did have two soldiers with me who came from that house. Which ones were they? I can't remember. I was too wrapped up in my own head to note their names or faces.

"I have one more thing for you." He reaches into the breast pocket of his jacket and pulls out a single sheet.

"I don't want anything else," I say when he holds it out to me.

"The doctor who looked after you when you were in the coma, did you know he died a few days after you woke?"

I glance up at him, confused. I hadn't even thought about that. I'd been introduced to another doctor. I'd assumed he was the one who'd looked after me.

"Drove off a bridge in the middle of the night," he says. "A bridge about eighty miles from his house in a town he had no ties to. Absolutely no connections, no reason to be there."

"What are you saying? If you're accusing David, you and I both know he doesn't do that sort of work."

"No, he has others do it for him. Why don't you talk to Lenore?"

"What does Lenore have to do with anything?"

"She came to me once. Years ago. She was worried about the drugs they were giving you to keep you in the coma."

"They did that so I would heal. It's detailed in the medical reports."

"By a doctor your uncle employed who was subsequently killed in a strange sort of *accident*."

No. Uncle David wouldn't have done that to me.

"I wish I were wrong, Cristiano." He finishes his whiskey.

I bow my head, letting my eyes focus on the papers before me.

"You read through those. Let's talk tomorrow, make a plan."

I nod once, sit back down and skim one of the reports. Charlie's thorough. He's always been thorough.

It's the reason he worked for my father and one of the reasons he works for me. The other reason is that I trust him. He may not be blood, but I've always trusted him.

But if I believe him now, then my own blood has betrayed me.

No. It's not possible. Uncle David's been like a father to me since the murders.

Charlie walks to the door. "Cristiano," he says.

I look up. I'm tired. I'm so fucking tired.

"I'm sorry," he says.

I don't say anything. I just let him walk out the door.

16

CRISTIANO

My steps are heavy as I make my way below ground. The flashlight illuminates the path ahead of me, but I don't need it. I know the underground of this house. It's not only the cells that are down here.

I bring the bottle of whiskey to my mouth and swallow two mouthfuls as thoughts swim in the chaotic sea of my mind.

The voices from that dream. Were they Lenore and Uncle David? I recognize the scent of the aftershave. It's my uncle's. Something he has custom made. But was the other voice Lenore's? What had she said? Why can't I fucking remember what she said?

I drink more, the liquid sloshing in the bottle.

It's cold down here. And damp. If I close my eyes and stand very still, I swear I can feel the sea pressing against the rock. No. That's not true. Not yet. That only happens in the tunnel.

I walk to the farthest cell. The one where Scarlett's brothers were killed. I shine the light through the bars to see the dark stains in the stone floor. Evidence of their deaths.

If my family had gotten down here the night of the massacre, they'd be alive.

But we'd been ambushed. We'd had no chance.

The heavy door creaks as I push it open. There are two cells down here. I guess it was a fifty-fifty chance my uncle would have put the De La Cruz brothers in this one. Even he doesn't know about the tunnel.

I walk to the far corner where the carcass of an old mattress rests. That was here before I was. I don't know why I know that. Don't know if it's true knowledge, some memory I haven't lost, or my mind playing a trick on me. This part is almost as bad as not remembering them. I don't trust myself. Don't trust my own thoughts.

I shove the mattress away. It's light and something scurries from underneath it. I search the stones behind it and sure enough, I see it. The false stone.

Laying the flashlight down I set my hands on it, feel the smooth surface. Even though it's made to look like the others, there's a textural and a temperature difference.

I Thee Take

Like I knew of the stone's existence, I also know how to access the tunnel behind it. Because this false rock is a doorway. A secret way on and off the island.

A memory comes then, sharp as a blade. Blinding as a bolt of lightning. It hurtles into me at once and I hear a crash, feel liquid splash my legs.

Michael, Dante, me and dad. We're young, I'm eleven which makes Michael twelve and Dante ten. My father is holding Dante's hand and mine. Michael is too grown up for it, always wanting to show how brave he is. He wants to make Dad proud. We all do.

"Your brothers are too young. This is our secret, just us," my father says. "Michael, it'll be your job to look after it one day. To tell your brothers." Elizabeth wasn't born yet, I realize. I wonder if her birth was planned or a happy accident.

He pushes the rock out of its place and there, behind it is a black hole.

"And Cristiano, you'll help him. You'll be his right hand." He looks down at us, making a point to stop so we are looking up at him. "You're blood. Never forget that blood matters, boys."

Michael and I both nod.

"What about me?" Dante asks.

My father ruffles the hair on his head. "You'll help them too, but there's plenty of time for that. You just be a kid a little longer."

We turn to look into the dark hole. I pull back

but he shines his flashlight inside, and I can see that it's a tunnel. Just a few feet inside is a shelf stocked with flashlights, batteries, even canned food and bottles of water. There is also a pistol and several rounds of ammunition.

"It leads to the mainland. But it's eight kilometers long so you'd better have on good shoes," he says, and he lets go of my hand to unpack the bag he brought down with him. Inside it are supplies, food and fresh water to replace the expired bottles. New batteries to replace the old in the flashlights even though they still work. "Go on, boys. Not too far though. Dante you stay and help me."

I hear my brother whine about not being allowed to come with us as Michael and I take one of the flashlights and go exploring. It's a single long, deep tunnel, and it'd be pitch black if we didn't have the flashlight.

"I bet there are ghosts down here," Michael says.

"I know there are," I tell him. It's even colder in here than it was in that cell. We take a few more steps, even the sound of our breathing seeming to echo off the walls.

Michael turns to me. "You scared, little brother?"

I shake my head, but it's not true. I am a little scared.

"It's okay," he says, taking my hand. "I wouldn't let anything happen to you." His smile is kind, reassuring.

A few minutes later, Dad's flashlight bounces upon us.

I turn in time to see him, see his smiling face one more time before a sound catapults me out of the memory and into the present.

Before I can think, before my vision even returns, I act. Instinct. I lunge blindly at the shadowy form of whoever followed me down here. I hear a gasp, then air forced from lungs as I smash the intruder into the jagged, hard wall.

"Cr—"

I hear the gasp, but it takes me a long time to come back to the present. For my brain to make sense of who it is. And all that time I have her back to the wall, my forearm at her throat cutting off her air.

She makes a gurgling sound, and her hands fall away from my arm. She was clawing at me.

I look at her. At what I'm doing. I blink, draw back.

Scarlett.

Not a threat.

Just a Little Kitten who needs your protection.

Something crunches underfoot as I move back, shift my hands to her arms to keep her from dropping. I look down, smell whiskey, see the shattered glass, the liquid already absorbed by the stone.

Scarlett is coughing, almost doubled over. I return my gaze to her. I was choking her. I didn't even think. Just attacked. It's dangerous for her to be around me.

"What are you doing down here?" I ask, my voice hoarse, my mind split between past and present.

My father. Michael.

I want to see them again. I'd give anything to see them again.

At least Dante is alive. He needs you too.

"What are you doing down here?" I demand, angry now, shaking her. What else would I have seen if she hadn't interrupted?

Her eyes are wet and red when they meet mine.

"I needed to talk to you, and I saw you come down here."

I shake my head trying to clear the thoughts.

She coughs again.

"I didn't know it was you," I start, releasing her. I give her a little more space and run a hand through my hair.

She stares up at me and I wonder what I look like.

"Are you okay?" she asks me.

I look away from her, look into the tunnel.

Her gaze follows mine. "What is this?"

I walk a few steps into the tunnel and pick up one of the flashlights. It goes on instantly, the light it casts down the tunnel strong. I check the date on a couple of the cans of food, the water. All up to date. I wonder if Dante's been keeping the supplies fresh like our father had shown him. Like Michael should have been doing.

"Come here," I tell her.

She comes and it surprises me when I feel her little hand slip into mine.

"It's cold down here," she says, shivering, leaning into me a little. Her gaze is wide in the darkness that goes on for miles.

I watch her in that leftover, shadowy light of the flashlight. She shifts her gaze to mine as if she's oblivious to what she just did. "What is it?"

"Tunnel. It leads to the mainland. I just remembered it."

She stops walking. "What do you mean you just remembered it?" she asks, her forehead wrinkling.

I study her face in the dim light. Her whiskey-colored eyes. I feel her warm hand in mine and hold it tighter.

She trusts me. Whether she realizes it or not, she trusts me.

"Scarlett." I touch her cheek, tuck a strand of hair behind her ear.

Did my uncle give up her location? Did he know what they'd do to her? Is that why he came with me to rescue her? To keep an eye on things? He's never been involved in anything outwardly criminal. It had surprised me he'd wanted to come.

Her hand comes to my face and she wipes something off my cheek. We both look at her thumb and see the smudge of red. The small but sharp shard of crystal.

"What did you do?" she asks.

I lean in and kiss her. She's safe. She's here. Safe and warm in my arms.

"Cristiano?" she asks when I pull back.

"Doesn't matter."

I kiss her again and this time her eyes close and she kisses me back.

I set the flashlight on the shelf beside us, knocking two bottles of water to the ground. They make a *thump* then roll away into the pitch-black dark.

When she looks back up at me, I take her face in my hands and kiss her deeply. Sliding one hand beneath her top, I slip it up over her belly to cup her breast. She's not wearing a bra. She's in an emerald-colored slip. She must have just come out of bed.

I slide my hand lower into her panties as I deepen the kiss. My fingers weave through the mound of soft hair to cup her sex.

She moans into my mouth, hers going slack for a moment. I love how she responds to my touch. How she gives herself to me.

With my other hand, I undo my jeans, push them and my briefs down. I draw back to look at her, brush her hair back from her face again with both hands now.

"I need you," I say as she raises one leg to my waist.

I lift her up, so she wraps them both around me, the wall at her back and me at her front. I kiss her again while with one hand, I push the crotch of her panties aside and draw back a little to look at her as I take her.

She's wet. Ready. But the thrust still forces the air from her lungs.

Cupping her ass cheeks, I kiss her, watch her take me, our lips or tongues and teeth in constant contact. I listen to the wet sounds of our bodies coming together, hear our combined breaths sharp and broken with the thrusts.

She feels good. So fucking good. Warm and tight and like home. Like I belong here. Right here with her.

Here inside her.

"I'm going to come," she says against my mouth. "You're going to make me come."

Her mouth goes slack as soon as she says it. I hear her moan and feel her walls throb around me. When they do, I come too, letting the pulses milk me as I watch her. Beautiful Scarlett. Beautiful, scarred Scarlett.

My Scarlett.

I love her.

I know it in that instant. I know it as I empty

inside her. I know it as I hear the breathy whisper of my name on her tongue.

I love her.

And this moment, now, us here like this, it's honest and perfect while everything else is so utterly imperfect. While everything else is a lie.

Her legs go weak around me so I'm holding her up, kissing her as I draw out of her.

She's out of breath and sweat beads her forehead. I rest mine against hers. I'm breathless too.

"Everything is fucked up. Everything." I cup her face, kiss her cheek, never taking my forehead from hers as a tear slips from her eye.

"Shh." She cups my face too, wraps her arms around my neck and buries her cheek in the crook of my neck.

"Everything but you," I tell her but I'm not sure she hears.

17

SCARLETT

"What did you mean when you said you just remembered the tunnel?" I ask Cristiano, thinking how strange the statement had sounded. We're sitting in a hot bath after the episode downstairs. He's behind me and doesn't answer right away so I turn my head to look at him.

He meets my eyes. "I don't remember things."

"What do you mean?"

He looks thoughtful, far away, his forehead furrowed. "I don't remember things. People," he pauses. "I don't remember *them*, Scarlett."

"What?"

He shakes his head.

"I don't understand what you're saying," I say.

"When I woke up, I had no memory of anything

before the massacre. Nothing. Like the first seventeen years of my life didn't happen."

I feel my forehead wrinkle as I try to follow.

"I can't remember my own mother."

I'm trying to process, trying to make sense of this thing that makes no sense.

"None of them."

Something he said comes back to me then. When he gave me his mother's dress, he made the comment he'd given it to me to see if he'd remember. I hadn't understood what he'd meant.

"Oh, my God." I can't wrap my brain around the scope of it. He must feel wholly untethered. Lost. What does he hold on to when he has no past?

He shakes his head, moves to stand. I watch the water slide down over him, see the muscle, the scars, the tattoos. The wreck of the jagged script along his arm. I squint to read it, but no, that can't be right.

He wraps a towel around his hips then holds one out for me.

I stand and he wraps me in it, then lifts me out of the tub and carries me into the bedroom. I'm surprised again by how gentle he can be.

We stand at the edge of the bed as he dries the water from me.

"Do you remember the first day?" he asks. "When I brought you in here?"

I nod, trying to keep up when it often seems like he has half the conversation in his own head.

"You made me remember the Crème Caramel. My mother's. It was your eyes. They're the color of burnt sugar." He smiles but it's gone in a second. "You made me remember, Scarlett. That's never happened before."

"You have no memory of anything at all?"

He shakes his head. "I know every detail from the day I woke up from the coma to now. And that night. The night of the murders. That I can't forget. Can't stop seeing."

"Have you talked to a doctor or something?"

He gives a sad little laugh. It's more of an exhale. "No. No one can know. Well, apart from my uncle. And I think Lenore suspects."

"What about your brother?"

He shakes his head. "No. And he won't know. I can't let him down again."

"Let him down again?"

"He had to deal with it alone. I was in a fucking coma. May as well have been dead for all the good I did him."

"Cristiano, I don't think he'd—"

"He can't know, Scarlett. Ever."

I study him, but I don't argue this. Not now. "Maybe it's your brain trying to protect you or something. Maybe you should talk to someone. A professional."

"No. Drop it."

"But what if they can help? Maybe—"

"Drop it." He opens the towel to look me over and I know what he wants. I see it in the way his eyes have darkened. Feel it in the hardness that presses against my belly.

I lick my lips, open my mouth to say something but he leans down to kiss my lips, the curve of my neck, the shell of my ear.

One hand slips down my back over the curve of my hip to cup my ass. His kiss deepens and he slides his hand over. A moment later, I'm on tiptoe, my eyes wide open.

He looks at me but doesn't move his hand. His fingers.

"I want this," he says, watching me as his fingers play with my back hole.

"Cristiano."

"Turn around," he whispers.

"I—"

He turns me, not giving me a chance to comply. Sliding his hand up between my shoulder blades, he bends me over the bed.

"I haven't looked at you like I want," he says, crouching behind me.

"Cristiano," I start, moving to straighten.

He stretches a hand between my shoulder blades. "Stay."

"I—"

But he lays the tip of his tongue on my sex and I gasp.

And stay.

With his hands on my thighs, he spreads my legs wider then sets them on my cheeks to splay me open. Dipping his head, he reaches his tongue to my clit before licking the length of my pussy up to my other hole, then back.

Embarrassed, I begin to pull away.

"I said stay," he repeats, low and commanding.

Again, I stay.

"You're very responsive. Always wet for me." His tongue teases me, dips inside me then circles my other hole again. "But this right here," he starts, straightening to stand and keeping one hand on my ass while opening the nightstand drawer with the other. "This I haven't had a chance to make mine yet."

I swallow, liking his dark eyes on me, liking how big he is, how much bigger than me. How much in control of me he is like this.

He gives me a lop-sided grin and opens the tube of what I guess is lotion or lubricant. I hear the pop then feel the cool sensation of it as he squeezes it onto my lower back.

"What are you doing?"

"Making you mine. Every part of you."

"Cristiano, I don't think—"

"Down." His hand splays between my shoulder blades. "I've taken your pussy. I've taken your mouth.

But I haven't taken your ass yet and I want to, Scarlett."

I shift my gaze to his cock and panic has me trying to straighten again. "You can't put that in there."

"Why not?"

"Because…I…well, because…" I don't know. "It won't fit," I blurt.

He laughs outright at that. "You're good for me, you know that? You make me laugh."

"I don't think it's a laughing matter. I really—"

But he leans down over me to kiss the corner of my mouth, swallowing the rest of my words. "Don't worry, I'll make it fit," he says, and, eyes on me, smears the lotion around and then into me.

I gasp, every muscle tightening.

"Relax," he says.

I try. It doesn't hurt. It's just I've never had anything in there.

"Okay?" he asks.

I nod as he moves his finger slowly in and out while the fingers of the other hand slip between my legs to tease my clit.

"Good little Kitten," he says, and I lay my head down and close my eyes and feel. "Just relax, Kitten. We'll go slow. There, like that, does it feel good?"

I nod, eyes still closed.

"Open your eyes and look at me."

I do and with two fingers of one hand deep

inside me, he guides his cock to my pussy with the other.

"You're tight. Tighter now," he says as he dips inside me once, twice.

I moan, arching my back, wanting more. "I want to come."

"Not yet." He pulls out and I watch him fist his cock again, jerking it. I see the little drops of precum on the thick, rounded head and I find myself biting my lip, wanting it. Wanting him to watch me. To touch me. To take me like this.

"I think you're ready," he says pulling his fingers out and placing his cock at my back entrance.

I place my hands on the bed, back ramrod straight. "Wait! I—"

"Relax. Lay back down. I want to take this last piece of you. Don't you want to give it to me?"

I'm not so sure.

"I want to feel you come with my cock in your ass, Scarlett. And you're going to come hard. I promise." As he says it, he presses in. He works slowly, taking his time, stretching me. When he slides his fingers to my clit, I begin to moan.

It feels good, really good. And he's giving me just enough to keep me on the edge of orgasm, pulling his fingers away when I'm close, claiming more of me as I relax.

"It feels good," I manage.

I hear rather than see his satisfied smile "I'm

almost all the way inside you. Just a little more. Give it to me, Kitten. Push against me and let me have you."

I do. I want to. And so, I close my eyes and do as he instructs, and I know a few moments later when he's fully seated inside me by the deep, low moan that comes from his chest. I look back to watch him as he watches me.

"Christ. I wish you could see how you look. How beautiful you are stretched around me like this."

I slip my fingers between my legs. "I want to come."

"Greedy little Kitten. Come," he says, beginning to move inside me, slow at first, then faster as he shifts one hand between my legs to cover my own. Our fingers are wet as we stroke that hard little nub and only moments later I come apart, my body pure sensation, pure ecstasy.

"Fuck," he mutters. "You are so tight."

He makes a sound that seems to be ripped from his chest. He grips my hips and takes me in long, deep strokes as he holds me tight the sensations different than anything I've ever felt making me come again, slipping from one orgasm to the next as I watch him watch me. As he takes one more piece of me. As I belong to him in one more way.

"Cristiano!" I call out, collapsing breathless and worn out as he thickens and throbs and empties, my body pure sensation, my awareness only of him. Him inside me. His weight on top of me. Him.

And I know this is where I belong. I never want to be without him again.

Because I think I love him.

18

CRISTIANO

I find Lenore in the kitchen the next morning.

"Good morning," she says, looking me over as she wipes her hands on the apron. "Didn't you sleep well?"

I must look like I feel. After Scarlett fell asleep, I lay awake beside her listening to her breathe, feeling her small, warm body beside mine. Watching her. In a way, it surprises me how easily she falls asleep with me. There's a level of trust she may not admit to because sleep is the ultimate vulnerability.

And you were asleep for six years under Uncle David's care.

I shove that voice away. It's one that's come before. It's the one that thought adding my uncle's name to my reaper's list was a good idea. I need to talk to him because part of me can't reconcile the uncle I know with the man Charlie would have me believe he is.

What if it's true? What then?

"I'm fine," I say to Lenore.

What would it change if it were true? I have to stay the course. Find Marcus Rinaldi. Find out what he said to my mother. Then kill him. It doesn't matter if my uncle has used me to punish his enemies, does it? Nothing matters but avenging my family.

"Sit with me," I tell Lenore when she hands me a cup of coffee.

"I have to make the—"

"Sit with me." I pull out a chair.

"Well, all right." She sits.

I sit across from her and Cerberus comes to lounge beside me, resting his head on my shoe. He trusts me too, like Scarlett.

"I remembered something the other night."

She tilts her head, waiting for me to continue.

"I remembered waking up. Or almost waking up."

"What do you mean, Cristiano?"

"I think you know that my memories are gone."

She lowers her lashes, but nods, then turns her gaze back to mine. "Maybe in time—"

"No. That's not what I want to talk about."

"Oh. Okay."

"I was waking up. I think I was, at least. From the coma, I mean." I study her, watch her shift her position in her seat. "I think it was your voice. You said something about damage. Permanent damage. Uncle David was there. I recognized his aftershave."

She's on her feet in an instant, moving to the stove, opening it. "I'm sure it was a dream."

I stand too, go to her. "I'm pretty sure it wasn't." I close the oven door and take her arm, turn her to face me.

Her eyes are wide, wet.

"The doctor who treated me, I didn't know he'd been killed."

"Cristiano, don't."

"Tell me about the damage. Tell me what you knew."

She shakes her head. "There's nothing to tell."

"There's something and we both know it."

She looks down to Cerberus, who whines, then back up at me.

"You're like a grandmother to me. You always have been. I need you to tell me the truth, Lenore. I have so few people in my life that I can trust."

"I just..." she shakes her head, breaking off, wringing the towel in her hand. "He...they kept you comatose for so long."

"Go on."

"You were fighting to wake up. You almost did a

few times." She stops, shakes her head and she won't look at me when she continues. "But I'm not a doctor. I don't understand these things and they said you needed the time to heal."

The morning my brother found me I was close to death. The coma had been induced to help me heal. This six-years long sleep.

"But you didn't think I needed that time?"

"I don't know, Cristiano. I just know you tried to wake up. I saw it a few times myself. Felt it when you squeezed my hand."

She could be wrong. That squeezing of the hand, isn't that just the body's muscles working without direction from the brain? She's right, she's not a doctor. And neither am I. All I've had to go on is what I've been told and all I could do was trust it to be the truth.

"What did my uncle say to you the other night?" I ask, changing direction.

She looks down, then pushes the heels of her hands into her eyes.

"What did he say, Lenore?"

It takes her a full minute to look back up at me.

"He said it could have been worse for Alec." She wipes her face which is wet now with tears.

My jaw tenses. My hands fist and relax. "And how did you think he meant that? As a comfort?"

"Don't ask me that, Cristiano. Do not ask me that.

My nephew was shot twice protecting your wife. That's all I know." She shifts her gaze away from mine at that last part.

"Do you resent Scarlett for that? Blame her somehow?" I ask because I hear her tone and it's not the first time she's said something that has made me question.

She closes her eyes, shakes her head and takes a long time to open them again. "No, Cristiano. I don't even know why I said that. She's innocent. I know it."

There's more. I see it in her worried expression. "If you're afraid, know that I'll keep you and Alec safe. I promise."

"He wasn't safe that night."

I grit my teeth, take a deep breath in. She's right. "It won't happen again. I'll lay my own life down before I let anyone hurt you or Alec."

"No, that's not…I love you like I love him. Like I loved my daughter. Like I loved Mara. *Love* her," she corrects. But she's wavering now between past and present. Loved. Love. Has she given up hope after all these years?

Her eyes fill up again and I see so much sadness, but she wipes it away and forces an almost smile. "I'm an old woman, but Alec, he's so young."

"I promise, Lenore."

She nods, looks down at the floor then walks backward to sit down.

"The medicine they were giving you to keep you in the coma, I asked about it. I asked your uncle, and I asked another doctor and did a little research. Maybe I shouldn't have. I could have put you in danger. I know that."

"What did you learn?"

"David knew if it was used for a prolonged period, it could—*would*—cause permanent memory loss."

He knew?

The door opens then and Antonio walks in. He stops just inside the door.

Lenore and I both turn to look at him.

"We've got a problem," he says.

"What is it?"

"Dante."

My heart drops to my stomach. "Is he okay?"

"For now. But we need to go."

I nod and as I cross the kitchen, I think about them all. All the people who need me to keep them safe. Scarlett. Lenore. Alec. Dante. Even Cerberus needs me. So many people depending on me and what have I wanted all this time? Vengeance. And then? And then death. I won't deny that anymore. It's selfish. I'm selfish.

But maybe in my case, dead is better.

I'm just about to walk out of the kitchen when Lenore calls my name. "Cristiano."

I stop, turn.

"He knew," she says. "They gave you more of those drugs when you started to wake up to keep you asleep. He knew all along. And that doctor," her expression is one of disgust. "That doctor was on his payroll."

19

CRISTIANO

"Where is he?"

Antonio and I are on the chopper along with two soldiers.

"I know one of the officers. He took him home. No arrest was made."

"Where the fuck were the soldiers he's supposed to have with him at all times?"

Antonio ducks his head to look out onto the water as we near our landing spot.

"He doesn't take them with him. Hasn't in a while."

"What?"

"As soon as he gets to the mainland, he drops them."

"What do you mean he drops them?"

Antonio takes a deep breath in as the chopper lands then turns to me. "He's doing something, and I can't figure out what it is. I have the men tail him but there have been a few times we've lost him."

"And you haven't thought to mention this to me?"

"You've got a pretty full plate, Cristiano."

"My brother takes priority." We climb out of the chopper and walk across the lot to the waiting SUV. "What's he doing?"

"He's looking for someone. I don't know who but it's a girl."

I look at Antonio. "A girl?"

He shrugs a shoulder. "He puts on a good face for you, but your brother's got demons. And he's self-destructive."

Family trait.

"I know about the demons." I hear him at night. The nights he sleeps at the house that is. The nights he sleeps. "I don't care what happens but from now on, you double the men on him. Give him space but you can't lose him. Period." *I* can't lose him.

Antonio nods and we ride in silence the rest of the way to a small, non-descript house along the outskirts of the city. Soldiers secure the perimeter as Antonio and I make our way to the front door. We don't have to ring the bell. The woman who lives here, I'd guess the wife of the man who kept my brother out of jail, opens the door, her expression one of worry.

She meets my eyes for a split second, mutters

something under her breath and makes the sign of the cross before stepping aside, almost disappearing behind the door.

"Christ," a man's voice says as I look around the small living room with its low ceiling, the tiny kitchen with a kettle on the stove that's whistling. I watch the man walk into the kitchen to switch off the burner and move the kettle. He gives his wife an irritated look before turning to me and Antonio.

He's middle-aged with a slight paunch to his belly. He's still wearing his police uniform.

"Antonio," he says, shaking hands with him before turning to me, giving me a nod.

I extend my hand to shake his and he smiles, puts his hand in it.

"Cristiano," I say.

"Emil. Emil Giordano. Pardon my wife." He has an accent, like he comes from a rougher part of the town.

"No, nothing to pardon," I say as we watch her close the door then disappear into the kitchen. "It's early and we come unannounced."

He half-shrugs his shoulder. "This way," he says, gesturing for us to follow him through the living room and down a hallway to the last door.

"Can you tell us what happened?" I ask.

"He got into it with a couple of guys at a bar in town. Not the best place to begin with. There were six of them against your brother. I gotta say, he held his own for a time but six against one aren't good odds. Thing is, he started it and the bar owner knows the others. I recognized Dante. I remember what happened to your family. Terrible thing to go through."

"Thank you," I say, trying not to feel any emotion.

"I told my partner I'd take care of it, but we had to make like we were arresting him. Your brother is a little bent out of shape because of it."

"He'll get over it. Your partner?"

"Don't worry about him. I paid him a couple bucks."

I nod. "Antonio will take care of you. I'd like to see my brother."

"Sure thing."

The man opens the door to the little bedroom. It's about the size of my closet with a single bed pressed to the far corner and a nightstand with a lamp on it.

Dante is just sitting up when I walk inside and close the door behind me.

"You smell like a brewery."

"Distillery," he corrects, his voice hoarse and scratchy. "It's whiskey."

"My bad."

He looks up at me from his seat on the edge of the bed. "Can you close that?" he asks, shielding his face. The morning sun coming through the window is a glare in his eyes.

"Hungover?" I ask, pulling the ropes to close the broken blinds. "Or are you still drunk?" I turn back to him.

He looks up at me and I see the bruise forming along his jaw, see the cut on his lip and the blood on his knuckles.

"The latter," I guess. "How do the six men you picked a fight with look?"

He grins but winces, touches a cut high on his cheekbone. "Like shit."

I sit down beside him. "What the fuck, Dante? You have soldiers. Why were you alone?"

A darkness I don't like, but recognize, shadows his features. "There's some things I have to do alone, Brother."

"Like try and get yourself killed?"

"Unlike you, I wasn't trying to get myself killed."

The way he says it strikes me. Maybe my brother is more intuitive than I realize. "What were you doing at that place anyway?"

"Nothing." He shakes his head.

"You just said yourself there's some things you need to do alone. What are they? Is it those things that have you off the island so much? That have you coming back stinking of whiskey the mornings after?"

He runs a hand through his hair, turns to me. His

hair's a shade lighter than mine and sometimes, at some angles, he looks like mom in that portrait.

"I leave you to deal with Rinaldi. Leave me to deal with this."

"What exactly is *this*? Tell me and maybe I'll leave you to handle it."

"Haven't you got enough to keep you occupied? Maybe keeping an eye on your new wife and her brother? Enemies you've let have the run of our home."

"They're not our enemies."

He snorts, shakes his head and looks toward the window with the slivers of light still coming in from the old-fashioned blinds that don't quite close correctly.

"Do you ever wonder what happened to Mara?" he asks.

I'm taken aback but only miss a beat. "Of course, I do."

"Do you wonder if she's still out there? All alone?" he looks at me when he asks this part and I see my brother as a kid, uncertain, not cocky, not tough. Just unable to make sense of what happened. "Do you wonder if she needs us and we're just here getting on with our lives? Forgetting her? Forgetting them?"

"We're not exactly getting on with our lives, are we?"

"You know what I mean."

"Why is this coming up now?"

"The kid, Noah, he had a picture of her."

"Noah? Why would he have a picture of her?"

"He'd taken one out of Lizzie's room and he was talking to Scarlett. I walked in on them and I don't know. I didn't like it. It just got me thinking again if she's still out there and helpless. They were five, Cris. Fucking five years old. How the fuck do you hurt a five-year-old kid?"

I look away. I can't see his pain. It wounds me every time I get the slightest glimpse of it. Cuts right through me.

"You want to know what I was doing?" he asks, abruptly getting to his feet.

I remain seated and nod.

"I was looking for the girl. The one who called me that night. Who told me to come out. I'd met her a few days before at a club and I didn't expect her to call but she did. And like a selfish ass I went out and…" he trails off, turning his back to me. "You know how I spent the night my family was being massacred?"

I get to my feet. "Don't do this."

"No." He turns to me and I see something I recognize in his eyes. Hate. Self-hate. "I should do it. I should own up to it."

"It wasn't your fault you weren't there. And if you had been, what the fuck for? To die? To fucking die?"

"I was getting my dick sucked for the first time.

That's what I was doing while you were being attacked. While you were being slaughtered like fucking animals." I hear grief morph into rage at the last part. Grief turned into pain and rage.

I take a breath in, try to keep steady because he needs me to keep steady. To be the foundation, the rock he can rest on.

The room is so small, it only takes two strides to get to him. I put my hand on his shoulder. "What happened wasn't your fault."

"I'm not saying it was. I just...I don't fucking know." He shoves my hand off and turns back to the window. It's quiet for a long minute. "Do you sometimes wish you'd died with them?"

It takes me a long time to answer. "I used to. But then I'd get angry. I'd make myself see Rinaldi, see him with the knife at mom's throat."

I don't tell him the other part. Dante doesn't know what Rinaldi did to her before he killed her. I hadn't realized my uncle knew but I guess it makes sense. Any medical examiner would have known and told him.

Dante turns to look at me.

"I'd think about that and I'd think about why I survived. And it gives me strength. Strength I needed to wake up and get out of bed for a long time. I will avenge our family. I will not rest before that happens."

"What about Scarlett? You chose her over that

vengeance."

Now it's my turn to shift my gaze away as I rub the back of my neck. "Scarlett has complicated things."

"How?"

Fuck.

I face my brother but don't quite meet his eyes. "I'm in love with her."

It's the first time I say it out loud. First time I really hear it. Understand it.

I focus on my brother's eyes. I can't tell what he thinks at hearing this. His features are schooled, steady, we're both good at that. He studies me and I let him. It's all I can do. Because this is the truth, and he deserves the truth.

He nods, turns his gaze downward. I think how he's sobered up since I first walked into this room.

"I know you don't like or trust her. I understand. But I know she's as much a victim as our family was."

He shifts his gaze back to mine. "What if she's not who you think, Cristiano? What if she betrays you?"

"She won't."

"What if she does?"

Something twists inside my chest. "Then I'll deal with her," I say, my voice tight.

"What if you don't make it to deal with her?"

I steel myself. It won't happen, I tell myself.

"What if you don't make it to deal with her?" he asks again a little more forcefully.

"It won't come to that."

"What if it does?"

"You don't touch her. You don't lay a finger on her. Whether I'm dead or alive. You protect her."

He snorts.

I grab his shoulder. "You. Protect. Her."

His eyes narrow.

"For me," I say.

Nothing.

"Promise me, Dante. Promise me if anything happens to me, you'll protect her. Keep her safe."

Gazes locked, we stand quiet for a long moment. She won't betray me. I know that.

Dante nods tightly once and it's in that moment I truly grasp that my brother is a man. And that he is capable. And that he is capable of violence. Because his nod wasn't his acquiescence. The opposite.

If something happens to me, he'll punish Scarlett. I know it.

If I die, she dies.

It will not come to that.

"I'm looking for the girl," he says. I'm confused. He must see it because he continues. "From that night."

"Why?"

He sighs. Shrugs his shoulders. "She disappeared. When I called the number she gave me, it was disconnected. When I went to the apartment I thought was hers, it was empty. I was drunk. So fucking drunk but this thing it's fucking with me, Cris. It's making me doubt my own memories."

He's not alone in that.

I watch him, watch the confusion in his eyes. See the self-doubt that is too familiar. I wrap a hand around the back of his head and tug him to me. We hug. We haven't hugged in a while.

"We'll figure it out. Together. Okay? We'll figure this shit out."

He gives me a smile when I pull back. "I should apologize to the cop. I was an asshole."

"Yeah. You should. I'll make sure he's paid well but you should." I open the bedroom door and we step into the hallway. "Question for you. Are you keeping the supplies in the tunnel up to date?"

He smiles. "Yeah. I have been for a while. Dad said it was you and Michael who'd have to do it but you couldn't so the task fell to me. You went down there?"

I nod. "Does anyone else know about it?"

He shakes his head. "No way. Dad said just us."

"How'd you get there?"

"I'd come in from the other side when we were in hiding."

"So Uncle David doesn't know either?"

"No."

"Good. Keep it that way. Let's go home."

20

SCARLETT

Cristiano closes the door and sits on the couch. He returned to the island an hour ago with his brother who looked a little worse for wear.

I take a seat beside him.

"What's going on?" I ask.

He scrubs his face then takes Cerberus's eager one into his hands. He looks at the dog who makes a whining noise as if he feels his master's agitation.

I hear one of Cristiano's signature grunts as he turns his attention to me and pets Cerberus absently.

"You remember how to move the rock to get into the tunnel?"

I nod. He just showed me last night.

"If anything happens to me, you go. Take your brother and go."

"What?"

"Keep Cerberus by your side as long as you can. He'll protect you." He gets up, goes to his desk and opens a drawer to take out a pouch. He holds it out to me.

I take it and feel the jagged edges of whatever is inside, the weight.

"There's cash in there and information on the bank account where there's more. It's in your new name. Everything you need to disappear is inside including new passports. If anything happens, you call Charlie. He's the only one you call, do you understand?"

I unzip the bag, look inside it, look back up at him. "Cristiano—"

"I put his name and—"

"I don't want a gun," I say as I look inside to find a small pistol, more cash than I can count, two passports and a key.

"Noah will handle the gun. The car is at the dock where you'll exit the tunnel. The information—"

"Cristiano." I walk around the desk, set the pouch on top of it and take his face in my hands, making him look at me. "What the hell are you talking about? What happened that you're giving me this?"

He takes a deep breath in and just looks at me for a long minute. "I love your eyes, you know that?"

"What happened with your brother?"

"They're so expressive. So open."

He's distracting me but the look in his, something about it breaks my heart. "Only for you."

He smiles at that but it's a sad smile. "In your eyes I see the real you. I see inside to your soul. And I feel your heart, Scarlett." He puts the flat of one hand over my heart and takes hold of mine to place it over his. "I feel you."

He leans down, kisses my mouth, then pulls me into his chest, trapping my hand between us as he wraps his arms around me. He lays his lips on my forehead before cupping the back of my head to hold me against him and rests his head on top of mine. "I didn't think this would happen. And now of all things. Fuck my timing."

I draw back, look up at him. "You didn't think what would happen?"

He studies me for a long moment.

"What?" I push.

"I didn't think I would fall in love with a De La Cruz."

I'm startled. It takes me a long minute to process his words. That single word. Love.

My heart flutters, my belly doing a tumble and I'm still not sure I heard right. Not sure I understand. I reach up to touch the scruff of hair on his jaw. More than two days' worth now.

"Specifically, I didn't think I'd fall in love with stubborn as hell Scarlett De La Cruz." We look at each other, just look at each other. "I love you, Scarlett."

"I love you, too, Cristiano."

He wipes away the tear that slips from my eye. I see the shadows under his, dark like he hasn't rested in days. Years.

"You didn't sleep."

He shakes his head.

"What happened with your brother?"

It's cold when his arms fall away from me. He steps back, sits in his chair and sighs deeply. "I have more enemies than I can count."

I sit on his lap and slip my hand into his. He takes it, intertwines his fingers with mine and looks at our bound hands.

"I'm not your enemy. And I'm not going anywhere without you, Cristiano," I say, studying him in profile.

His gaze meets mine. "If it comes to it, you are." He sets me on my feet and stands up again. He's anxious, I feel it. "I want to show you something," he says and, keeping my hand in his, we leave the study. We stop to put on jackets before walking out of the house and into the overcast, windy day.

"I need to talk to you actually," I start, almost forgetting the reason I needed to talk to him.

"Later," he says, keeping hold of my hand as we climb the steep rocks to the west of the island. The wind is stronger here and I duck my head against it, shivering in the cooler temperature as clouds overtake the sun completely.

"Where are we going?" I ask once we've crested the hill. The wind is stronger here. Almost violent. I have to keep pushing the hair off my face and I won't let go of his hand for fear I'll be blown away.

"There," he says.

I see what he's pointing to a little distance ahead of us. My mouth falls open because there, built into the rock face is a mausoleum.

"It's carved into the stone," he starts as we reach the foreboding front face. "The façade is marble. My grandfather added on to it. You can see the difference in the veining. He couldn't get exactly the same."

"I've never seen anything like this." It's large, taking up the entire side of the rock here. And I can see where the addition was made. It's beautiful and eerie at once. "Is it always this windy up here?"

He points to the darker clouds in the distance. "There's a storm coming." We walk up the steps leading to the huge, metal door. He looks back down at me. "Are you scared?"

I look from the door up to him. "Not with you."

He smiles.

"But I wouldn't come up here alone in the dead of night or anything," I add as a sudden chill makes me shudder.

"That's wise," he says with a smile pulling me to

him momentarily, big hand warm on my back. "More for the cliff than the dead. You have nothing to fear from the ghosts of my family." He turns to the door before finishing the sentence and pushes it open. It's heavy. I can tell from the effort it takes. Cristiano ushers me inside as it creaks.

In here the air is different. There's a stillness almost as if the ocean isn't just beyond. Like the wind isn't attempting to blow us off the top of this cliff. And it's spotless. I guess I expected dust. Cobwebs. Creepy creatures in the darkest corners. But someone is taking care of the place. There's even a lamp that's burning a dim red.

"It's one of the first things I did," he says of the lantern. He releases my hand and walks toward the stone altar where the crucified Christ hangs overhead. I look up at him, make the sign of the cross.

He watches me, then shifts his gaze to wiping something off the altar, rearranging some of the things there.

"What are they?" I ask, stepping closer.

"My mom's rosary beads. They should have buried them with her but didn't. I don't know why. These are their wedding bands." He picks one up and turns it to read the engraving inside. Then hands it to me.

Inside is one word but it's in a language I don't know.

"What does it say?"

"Eternal, in my father's." He picks up the other one. "In my mother's, Love." He sets both back on the counter. "Latin."

"Should you leave them here? I mean, they're valuable."

"No one comes up here but me or Dante."

I look at the rosary. "Are those sapphires?"

He nods. "Lenore said dad had it made for mom. She kept them and only gave them to me when I woke up. And this is Elizabeth's favorite bear. She never even had a chance to wear it out."

I watch his hand fist around it. He turns away. From where I'm standing, I see his jaw tighten before he finally puts the stuffed animal down. It seems to take everything he has to do it, to release his fist, release his rage.

"What kind of monster kills a five-year-old girl?" he asks.

I touch his shoulder but have no words, so I lay my cheek on his back.

"Lenore stopped asking about Mara. I know she wants to every time she sees me but stops herself. Today, she mentioned that she loved her then corrected herself."

"I need to tell you something," I say.

"Past tense," he continues like I haven't spoken.

"Cristiano," I touch his shoulder. "There's something you need to hear."

He turns to me. "What is it?"

"When they killed my parents, Noah and I were separated for the first two years. They kept him in Mexico and brought me with them. He...the day of the wedding I was in your sister's room. Do you remember?"

He nods.

"Noah came there to see me."

"I'm not really following."

"While I was getting dressed, he must have been looking at the pictures. There was one in particular that caught his eye." I take a moment, look away as I consider. Should I tell him? What if Noah's wrong? What if he isn't but it's still too late?

"What is it, Scarlett?"

"I don't want to get your hopes up."

"What?"

"He could be wrong. I mean, it's been ten years and they were both so little."

His forehead wrinkles. He takes hold of my arms and squeezes. "Tell me."

"He recognized one of the girls. Elizabeth's friend."

"What?"

"Someone had written the names of all the little girls on the back."

"That's what my brother saw? Noah with that photo?"

Should I be surprised Dante mentioned it? "Yes."

"He shouldn't—"

"He recognized her, Cristiano. He recognized Mara."

This stops him. "What?"

"He didn't know her name, but he knew her face."

Cristiano shakes me once. "What are you talking about?"

"He said they'd brought her to Mexico. He said Jacob had been fed up when she wouldn't stop crying and told him to play with her. Jacob told him her name was Elizabeth but he's pretty sure it was Mara from the picture."

"How?"

"You said Mara's body wasn't found. They left a mess. They wouldn't have hidden one body or disposed of one body. It makes no sense considering."

"What are you saying, Scarlett?"

"Is it possible they kidnapped Mara thinking she was Elizabeth?"

21

CRISTIANO

My head is swimming with thoughts of what Scarlett told me. Noah is off the island with some of the men, so I haven't been able to question him. I haven't told Dante or Lenore. I won't. Not until I can make sense of it myself.

Is it possible Mara's alive? Did they kidnap her thinking she was Elizabeth? To what end?

Blackmail? Who? They'd thought they'd killed us all.

But there's one thing that makes sense and the thought makes me sick.

I take a deep breath in. I need to stay focused on the task at hand. If Mara's alive, I will get her back. Bring her home.

"Sir," the soldier peeks his head into my uncle's

study. I'm sitting behind my uncle's desk looking through the photo album I found on it. "He's pulling in now."

"Thank you."

I turn the page on the album and look at more photos of my mom. My brothers and sister. None of my dad in this one, but he was gone a lot. More of my uncle in these than there are in the albums at home. I'm just closing the album when I hear him having an exchange with the soldier I left standing outside the study door. A moment later, the door opens, and my uncle stands framed in the light of the hallway.

He takes me in as I stand from his seat. I look him over, pick up the tumbler of whiskey and finish it. It's not my brand, but it'll do.

"What the fuck, Cristiano?"

"Close the door," I tell him.

"Oh, I should close the door to my own office behind me? I'll ask you again. What. The. Fuck?"

But he enters and closes the door.

"And where's Morgan?"

"Morgan?"

"The butler."

"Oh." I always forget his name. But seriously? A fucking butler? "He's having coffee." With my men in the kitchen for the last hour. I didn't want to lose the element of surprise.

My uncle's gaze shifts to the photo album on the desk. I pour us both a drink.

"Your brand is in the cabinet underneath," he says.

"This will do." I hand him his and lean on the desk as he takes a seat on the armchair along the wall.

"What's going on?"

"I didn't know the doctor who had treated me all those years had been killed."

"Excuse me?"

"The doctor. When I was in the coma."'

"Oh, him. Yeah, it was tragic. I heard about it the morning after it happened."

"Why didn't you mention it?"

"You had more important things to worry about. Besides, I found you a new doctor. Why are you here? Like this? What's this about, Cristiano?"

"Did you know the drug he gave me would cause me to lose my memories?"

He exhales, shakes his head and sips his drink. "It was a possibility, yes. I knew that. But it was the only option. Your life was what mattered at that point. You were barely holding on. Did you want me to take a chance with your life when your brother was counting on you?"

Guilt. I drink more whiskey. "I don't remember them," I say.

He sighs deeply. "It's possible you'll remember someday."

"I doubt it." I walk around the desk and open the album again to look at the photo of mom on her own. She's lying back on a pool chair, huge hat on her head, legs strewn over the arm of the chair as she reads. I get the feeling she didn't know she was being observed or that someone had taken the photo. She was always skittish when the camera came out. Said she didn't look like herself in pictures.

My uncle is beside me then. "She was a beautiful woman." He brushes dust I don't see off the image.

I shift just my gaze to study him, hearing something strange in his words, remembering what Charlie said.

Was I blind?

His eyes meet mine and for the briefest of moments, I see something foreign. Something cold.

But he blinks and it's gone. And he's the man he's always been to me. He smiles and the familiar lines crease the skin around his eyes. It's just my imagination.

"Sometimes it's better to forget, Cristiano."

"No, it's not."

"I'll tell you about her. About all of them."

"What did the couple you had me kill do to support the massacre of my family?"

"You mean the massacre of our family."

I wait for his answer.

"Let me show you," he says, moving around his desk to unlock a drawer. "I didn't want you to see these. I didn't want to bring up old pain. Forgotten pain. But someone's put a bug in your ear, and you're determined, I see."

He takes out a manila envelope, opens it to glance at whatever is on the first page before turning to me.

"Are you sure?" he asks.

I nod. My heart is racing, my gut twisted. But honestly, I don't know what he could show me that could overwrite what Charlie has shown me.

"Here." He hands over the envelope and sits down to rifle through the drawer again.

I sit, too, and look through the few pages. They're bank statements, several lines highlighted. The amounts transferred from one account to the other make up a generous sum. There's a photo before that. Several. They're of my father and the man I killed. They're arguing, it's apparent from the image. I check the date. It's a year before the murders. I compare to the date on the bank transfers. Three months prior.

"He and your father had a... falling out," my uncle says when I look at him. "When your father blackmailed him."

"Blackmail?"

He nods. "I told you, there was a reason I didn't give you these." He hands me the next folder. "I wouldn't want you to lose respect for your father."

Something dark tightens in my gut at his words. "My father didn't blackmail anyone."

"You didn't know the business yet, Cristiano. You were too young. Michael knew. Michael was being groomed."

I look through the next folder. Again, a transfer of funds to the same account as the previous.

"Your father wasn't the man you thought, perhaps. But maybe you forget that he was a criminal. As are you. He chose that life. As have you."

Something about how he says it hits me the wrong way. I'm not sure what it is, the tone or the words or maybe just the look in his eyes.

"Do you want to see more? Maybe Michael's involvement? He would have been your father's successor, after all."

"No." I close the folders and consider the evidence Charlie brought. Why hadn't he found these? He was thorough. He's always thorough.

"We need to take care with Dante now, Cristiano. Keep him out of that world."

At least we're in agreement there.

"Who turned you against me?" my uncle asks.

"It's not like that."

"Who?"

My phone buzzes in my pocket but I ignore it.

"Should I take a guess?"

The phone dings notifying me of a voice mail.

I finish my drink and set it down, reach into my pocket to take out my phone. "Do you think Alec tipped off Jacob to Scarlett's location?" I ask.

"You know I do. Everyone else died. Everyone was executed. That was sloppily done on his part. An amateur move."

"Why would he do it, though? What does he have to gain?" I ask him, phone in the palm of my hand.

"You should ask him that."

"Or do you think he was left alive to throw me off track? Send me barking up the wrong tree?"

He snorts, shifts his gaze to the photo album, closes it.

I look down at my phone. The name of the caller I missed flashes on the screen and for a moment I'm not sure I'm seeing it correctly.

My uncle starts to say something as I push the button to play the voice mail and bring the phone to my ear. Felix's accented voice and the pumping of blood against my ears drowns out my uncle's words.

"I have a location. He just got there but I'd hurry. He has a nickname, I'm told. The Minute Man." Felix chuckles. "The Rose Club. Back rooms. Where the real action is." The message ends.

My throat is dry. My uncle is still droning on. I

feel sweat already bead at my forehead. Feel my hands fist.

Without a word, I turn and walk out of the study and out of the house because tonight is the night Marcus Rinaldi dies.

22

CRISTIANO

The Rose Club is a high-end strip club for all intents and purposes. On the front end, at least. Four soldiers enter with me, flanking me.

Back rooms. Where the real action is.

The back rooms are where the more illicit events take place. Where drugs are sold. Where women are sold. Where those with more deviant desires are sated.

I stop just inside the deep velvet curtains that are so dark a violet they appear to be black. The lights are subdued, and three stages showcase three separate dancers. Two bars take up the whole wall at either end of the large room with glass shelf upon glass shelf of the highest quality liquor up to the vaulted ceiling. Throughout this room are situated richly upholstered deep violet chairs to match the curtains separating this room from the other spaces.

"He doesn't get out. Not tonight," I tell my men.

They all nod. I have two more men out front and two at every other possible exit.

"There." In the farthest corner I spot the two men who clearly don't belong here. They're standing on this side of a closed door, their jeans and T-shirts out of place. The ill-fitting jackets they are wearing, obviously borrowed, and the looks on their faces that of men who've never seen girls like this before.

He cannot be this stupid.

"Key," I say to the madam who is standing nearby.

"He's in the back rooms. I told you. I don't want trouble in here."

"I said key."

"Sir, I—"

I turn to her and she backs up a step when she sees my face. I lean toward her. She's five feet tall tops. "Key."

A moment later, the key card is in my hand. Modern, like a hotel room key.

I make my way through the center of the room to the door where the two men stand sentry. When they can drag their lecherous gazes from the women to finally notice us, they're too late to reach beneath their borrowed jackets before my men have disarmed them.

They start to speak in Spanish, words hurried, any loyalty Marcus thought he had gone.

"Take them out back," I tell my men, my eyes locked on that door. I hold the keycard up against the electronic pad and listen to the satisfying click as a green light blinks. I push the door open to find another corridor. The carpet, walls and ceiling are black. Sloppily done. No doors in this corridor. At the end, I come upon the second part of the club. The one the tourists don't see.

A security guard meets my eyes as he slips his phone into his pocket. I'm sure that was the madam announcing my arrival.

Without a word, he gestures to a door at the far end, then slips past me and into the corridor I just walked through.

My men and I cross the large, dimly lit space to the lone door at the far end. There, I use the same key card to enter.

Soundproofing must have cost a fortune in this place because I'm instantly assaulted by the sound of heavy metal music playing loudly. In the front room, the music is lighter, something the girls can dance to. I close the door behind me.

The downstairs room is large, open. Dark like the corridor. A set of stairs leads up to the second floor. I hear a man's laughter coming from the bedroom with the door ajar, followed by the sound of footsteps above. Whoever is descending won't see us before we see them but it's not Marcus. These men are speaking Spanish.

As soon as they get downstairs, my soldiers grab them from behind, guns to their temples. One is wearing a dirty tank top, the other a white T-shirt stained and stretched tight over his gigantic gut.

The two are surprised. Again, I wonder if Marcus is stupid or if this is a trap Felix set. I smile, put my finger to my lips as my men easily take hold of them and move them out the door.

I walk up the stairs, pistol at my side. I'm oddly calm. My heartbeat under control. My mind razor sharp and focused.

I hear a woman then. A woman's scream. It's muffled quickly and just for a moment, I have to stop because it takes me back. Takes me to my mom's screams. He didn't try to muffle those.

The bedroom door is open a crack and the large bed is across the room. A woman is lying on her back, arms stretched out to the sides, held by soldiers. They watch as Marcus, his hand over her mouth, has his way with her. I'm not sure if he paid for the act or if he's taking what he wants.

She's the first to see me. I know because her eyes go from wide to panicked.

Marcus's ugly ass bobs in my line of vision and it takes all I have to stay focused. To stay here. Because if I go back to the night of the massacre, I'll be powerless. I may as well be lying in a pool of my own blood again.

Without a word, I lift my weapon and point it between the eyes of the man to the woman's right.

Bang!

The woman screams but Marcus presses his hand harder against her mouth, unaware why she's screaming over the too loud music.

The man falls to the wall, drops into a chair there.

Marcus laughs the high-pitched insane laughter of the stoned.

The other soldier turns from his fallen colleague to me. I fire in the same instant his mouth opens. *Bang!* Red splatters against the wall behind him.

I see Marcus's head shoot up. He looks at the wall, then at the second man I killed. He shifts his gaze to the first one. His ugly ass has finally stopped its in out motion.

"What the—"

"Get up," I say.

He turns slowly to me and the woman beneath him scrambles off the bed. She falls to the floor, scurrying to collect her things, then runs out of the room and down the stairs.

"Keep her inside," I call out to the soldiers downstairs. I don't want her alerting anyone.

"Fuck!" Marcus scrambles too. Falling over the edge of the bed as I make my way around it. I know what he wants. The gun on top of his jeans. The idiot still has his T-shirt on but he's bare-assed.

"Move. Opposite wall." I point to the one farthest from the gun.

"My men are outside," he threatens.

"No, they're not," I say, taking his pistol and unloading it. I toss his jeans to him. "Get dressed. I don't need to see your dick."

He snorts, gives me a one-sided grin. I'm not sure if he's high or drunk or both. Maybe just plain old stupid. Which only reaffirms that he was not the brains of the operation that took down my family.

"Your mom sure liked my dick."

I breathe.

Slow. Steady. Deep.

Calm.

Stay calm.

Inhale.

Exhale.

I can't rush this. Can't kill him without finding out what he said. He's dying tonight. That's non-negotiable.

I keep my eyes on his as I raise my pistol to aim it at his now-limp dick.

"You want me to shoot it off before we get started?"

He puts up both hands, palms to me. His pupils are dilated. The fucker is stoned and stupid.

"Get fucking dressed."

He bends down to pick up his jeans and I watch him try to balance as he pulls them on. I see how dirty they are. How dirty the T-shirt is.

He's barefoot but I don't care about that. As soon as he's got his jeans on, I empty my gun of bullets and toss it aside, pocketing the ammunition.

Marcus looks confused.

I approach him but he doesn't move. Not at first. He's still looking at the discarded gun.

"I'm going to kill you with my hands," I tell him.

He lunges for the gun then even though it's useless.

I extend my leg and trip him. He goes down hard, slamming his face into the low wooden footboard of the bed.

"Fuck!"

"Idiot." I walk to him, get on one knee and turn him over, straddling him, but leaving his arms free. I want him to fight. I want this to last. I want his death to be a slow one.

The first punch sends his head to the side, blood spurting from his nose or mouth. I don't know, or care, which.

"Does it turn you on to hold them down, is that it?" I ask, hitting him again. The girls here are rented by the hour. "Tell me, bastard." I hit him again. "Can't get it up if they're willing?"

"Fuck you!" He stretches to his right and a

moment later, I take a hit to my temple with the butt of the emptied gun.

"That was my bad," I tell him as the room spins like the fucking cherries on a slot machine. He scrambles out from under me trying to get to the nightstand.

I reach him as he opens the drawer. I can see why he went there and not the door. Bullets. Fucker.

"Afraid to use your fists?" I ask him smashing his skull into the wall, pulling him back and doing it again before I release him.

He slides to the floor looking dazed, arms at his sides.

This isn't as satisfying as I thought it would be. It just feels sick.

"Tell me what you said," I say, taking him by the hair and pulling him up to stand.

"How's your girlfriend? Or is it wife by now? You like dipping your dick in my sloppy seconds?"

I smash my fist into his gut.

I have to remember why I'm here. I have to stay focused. If I get distracted, if I kill him before he tells me, I'll never know.

"Tell me what you said to my mother before you killed her."

"You know, you did me a favor. I never wanted that whore. Turned my stomach to look at her. At the lot of those fucking Mexicans."

I'm tempted to smash his head in again, but I

don't want to cause further brain damage before I get what I came for. Instead, I hold him upright, put my foot on his knee and push. Just a little. Just enough to get his attention.

"You're dying tonight, Marcus. It can be a very painful death. Or it can be slightly less painful. You know what hurts like a mother fucker?" Not that I know from experience. I've never felt it, but I have a pretty decent imagination for these things. I put a little more pressure on his knee and his eyes go wider. "You know your knees don't bend that way, right?"

"It wasn't me. I didn't want to do it," he starts blubbering like the fucking coward he is. "I fucking swear, man!"

I pull back a little, something cold running down my spine.

"Tell me what you said to her."

"He told me to do it. He said I had to make her watch. He told me who to kill first. Michael. He's the strongest."

"Was. He *was* the strongest."

"Make her husband watch. Make the bastards watch."

My hands are fisting, one in his hair, one at my side.

"Who? Felix? Was it Felix?"

He looks confused for a minute, then one corner of his mouth curves upward. "No, man. I don't fucking take orders from the fucking Mexicans."

"Then who?"

He studies me, his eyes seeming to clear a little. One corner of his mouth curves upward. He shakes his head and clucks his tongue. "You were supposed to die. You weren't supposed to live."

I put my foot back on his knee. "What. Did. You. Say. To. Her?"

"You want to know what I said to mommy?" he asks.

It's taking all I have not to kill him, but I push harder on his knee.

His eyes go wide. "You'll make it quick then? You swear?"

"I swear." Lie.

"I passed along his message. Just like he wanted."

The cold that just found its way down my spine fills my veins. "What. Message?"

"I told her David sends his regards."

The room goes silent. Or maybe it's the ringing in my ears that has drowned out all the noise. Whatever it is, I'm paralyzed. And it costs me because I hear the click first. I recognize what it is an instant before I feel the tear at my side, feel the cold of the blade as it cuts through skin and muscle as I hear what he said. As I make sense of it. As I understand.

Marcus grins.

I stumble backward, hand on my side, blood warm through my fingers.

"Back pocket," he says. "Always check the back pocket. That's a tip for you." He picks up his gun, loads some bullets. "Not that you'll need it."

I drop to the edge of the bed.

David? My uncle?

"David sends his regards." I hear it now. I hear him say it. I'd heard him then, too, but I couldn't remember or didn't want to remember.

My uncle was responsible? My uncle had my family slaughtered? My uncle had my mother raped?

"Oh, and one more thing."

I look up. Marcus is at the door.

"Your wife is a dirty whore. I may never have fucked her but let me tell you something. After seeing her take her *Uncle Jacob's* filthy dick, I really couldn't get it up for her anymore. That's some nasty shit."

He goes on but I don't hear any more words. Even his laughter is somehow tuned out. I'm not in control of my body anymore. It's not even instinct. It's rage. Pure, raw rage.

I'm across the room in an instant, the hilt of the blade from my side in my hand, a roar like that of an animal blotting out the heavy metal as I take him down, both of us landing heavy on the black floor in this back room.

Marcus's eyes have gone wide, the gun knocked from his hand with the impact.

I don't think. I don't breathe. I don't feel the pain of my wound as I hold his head down with one bloodied hand, leaning all my weight into it because I can't keep myself upright, as I raise my knife hand and bring it down into his jugular.

23

SCARLETT

Something's wrong. I feel it.

It's been hours since Cristiano left, and Noah still isn't back. I'm anxiously sitting in Cristiano's bedroom watching for either of them.

I glance at the pouch and the contents I've scattered on the bed. The gun looks ominous and I know it's for my own protection, but I don't want it. I don't want Noah to have it. I don't want either of us to have to use it.

There's ten thousand dollars in cash along with the two passports with our new identities. American passports. I have no idea if they're good forgeries or not, but I guess they are. The key is to a BMW.

Cerberus sits beside me looking out the window. He must feel it too, this anxiety. This feeling that something has gone wrong.

"Everything will be okay," I tell him. It's a lie. I have no idea if anything will be okay.

He sets his head on my lap with a small whimper.

Did Cristiano find Marcus? Is that why he's given me this pouch? Shown me the way off the island. I know this is the one thing that's kept him alive. His hate. His need for vengeance. The drive to kill Marcus Rinaldi. Does he still intend to be done with things now, though? Done with life once he's had his revenge? I know the passports didn't happen overnight. He's put some planning into it. But what's happened between us, hasn't that changed anything for him?

The sound of a speedboat has me running to the window. I'm not sure if Cristiano left by chopper or boat. I heard both earlier. I can't see who is on the boat before it disappears around the corner.

"Let's go," I tell Cerberus after shoving the money and passports back into the pouch and tucking it and the gun under my pillow.

My pillow.

How quickly I've come to call it mine.

Cerberus follows me out the door and down the stairs where I already hear Noah.

I breathe a small sigh of relief when I see him. He's talking with another soldier, someone I don't know, and the older man laughs at what he says. Cristiano is nowhere among the half-dozen men who enter, but Dante is. His eyes track me as I make my way to my brother.

I don't like Dante and I don't trust him. The feeling is mutual, I know.

"Scarlett," Noah says, coming to me. "Is he following you around now?" He points to Cerberus.

Dante glowers at me, pets Cerberus's head and passes us to the kitchen.

"I need to talk to you," I say as quietly as I can, so no one hears. As uncertain as I am about things, I do know one thing, I know what's best for my brother.

"Sure," he says, his face serious as he follows me up to Cristiano's room. "Did you tell Cristiano yet?"

I nod. "I'm not sure how he took it. He's processing, I guess."

Noah appears uncertain. "You think I'm remembering wrong? I've gone over and over it and I swear, the minute I laid eyes on the photo, I just knew. I felt it, Scarlett. Does he think I'm making it up?"

"No. No, of course not. That's actually not what I want to talk to you about." I take the pouch out from under the pillow but leave the gun where it is.

"What's that?" he asks.

"I have a bad feeling, Noah." I have these a lot and over the last ten years I've been right more often than wrong. Although maybe that was the circumstances. "Something's wrong. Something's happened. With Cristiano I mean."

He studies me. "No, don't worry. He'll be fine. He's got nine lives."

"How many of those has he used up do you think?"

He pauses at that and I think about how much he's seen, how much he's lived through for his fifteen years.

"What's in there?" he asks.

I take out his passport and hand it to him. He opens it and his eyebrows shoot up. "Michael Preston?"

I take out mine. "And his sister, Elizabeth." I know those names weren't random choices. I pull the pouch open so Noah can see the bills.

"Whoa."

I tuck my passport into my pocket. "Cristiano gave this to me. He said if anything happens, I'm to take you and go."

"Take me and go?" He looks confused. "Go where exactly? And how did he think you'd manage that? There are about two dozen soldiers on the island that I counted just on my way in."

"You're keeping count?"

"I'm not stupid, Scarlett. These men are loyal to Cristiano. If something happens to him and Dante takes over, I'm pretty sure you and I are dead."

"Shit." I sit on the edge of the bed, pushing my hand through my hair. I know this, but Noah saying it, Noah knowing it, it makes everything feel that much more dangerous.

Makes me doubly certain that I need him out of here. Now.

"Do you want to go?" he asks, sitting beside me. "I mean, would you? Right now? If we could?"

"Would you?"

He nods and I see the little boy he was when all this started. It's the look in his eyes he sometimes gets. Like he's just barely holding everything together. He's just fifteen. A kid. Even if he is taller than me and slowly starting to fill out. I see the little bit of a mustache he must have shaved a few days ago growing back in.

And what I'll have to do makes my stomach twist.

"He showed me a way out," I tell him, not answering his question. "A secret way."

"How? There's guards watching everything. It's an island, Scarlett. We're surrounded by water. There is no secret way."

"There is. Under the water."

"What?"

"There's a tunnel that leads off the island. Access is through the cell where they killed Angel and Diego. We just have to get to the cells."

"Wait. Why did they put us in there if there was a way out?"

"I don't think anyone but Cristiano knows about

it. Maybe Dante. Put that away, okay?" I motion to the passport. I don't want anyone walking in and seeing us with passports.

He looks down at it and tucks it out of sight in his back pocket.

"Here," I take out just a few hundred-dollar bills and push them into my pocket before handing him the pouch. "This too. There's a car waiting on the other side of the tunnel. Key's inside there. Don't be stupid with the car."

His eyes narrow as he takes the pouch. "I can drive just fine but why are you telling me all this now? You can tell me when we get there." He knows the answer. I can see it in his eyes.

"Because you need to go first, Noah. I'll follow as soon as I know he's safe."

"Scarlett—"

"I need to know he's safe."

"If he's safe, there will be no reason to follow."

"Then I'll bring you back. If we disappear together, they'll start a manhunt. As long as they see me, they won't think anything of you not being here. I'm his wife. I'm the one the cartel wants back."

"No. No way. I'm not leaving you behind. How will you protect yourself against them if he doesn't come back?"

I reach under the pillow and take out the gun.

He sucks in a breath, shakes his head. "No. No fucking way, Scarlett."

"Listen to me, Noah. This is my chance to get you out. This is our one real shot in all these years. And it may be the only one we get." I feel my eyes fill up with tears, but I steel myself, harden my heart. I will not be weak. I cannot. Not now. "I couldn't protect you against Angel and Diego but I'm not going to let anything else happen to you."

"What they did had nothing to do with you."

I don't want to discuss what our brothers did over the last ten years, so I put the gun back under the pillow. "Let's go. There's food and water if you're hungry and you'll need something warm." I walk past him into Cristiano's closet and take the warmest sweater I can find. A thick wool one that still smells like him.

Worry interferes in my thoughts, but I shove it away. There will be plenty of time to worry.

Noah's still standing in the same spot when I return but he's holding the pistol. I look at him and he looks at me and I rush to him, taking that thing from his hands, more determined than ever that this is the right thing to do.

"Here," I say, putting the sweater over his shoulders. I tuck the gun away.

"Scarlett. I don't want to leave you behind," he says, and I know from his tone that he'll acquiesce.

I smile. "It's okay. I'll be okay. And besides, you're not leaving me behind. I'm just coming a bit later."

Leaving Cerberus in the bedroom we walk out

into the hallway as casually as possible. We don't pass any guards upstairs, but I hear them downstairs. They move quickly through the living room and out the front doors. I hear the chopper a few seconds later.

"Let's go," I tell Noah and we hurry to the door that leads to the cells. I only remember how dark it is down here once we're through the door, but Cristiano thought of everything. There's a small flashlight in the pouch we can use to make our way down the stairs and hurry as quietly as we can to the last cell. I think we both try to avert out gazes from the dark stains on the stone floor where Diego and Angel died.

I take the flashlight from Noah's hand and pan it over the wall. Cristiano left the mattress slightly skewed and I find the boulder easily. Noah stays close behind and neither of us speak. I push on the boulder that is truly a door and after a few tries to find the right spot, it opens.

I smile, turn back to Noah whose eyes have gone wide.

"Here," I say, walking into the black hole to pick up one of the bigger flashlights and switch it on. It blinks twice but stays on.

Noah steps in behind me, taking the sweater off his shoulders and slipping it on.

"How long is it?"

"Eight miles. It's a straight shot."

Noah looks at me. "Come with me. Now. We can go now."

I shake my head, my eyes filling up again as I wrap my arms around my little brother. I can count the number of times over the past ten years that I've wondered if I'd ever see him again.

This time, the tears come, and I can't stop them.

"Give me two days. I'll be at the piazza. Under the tower. You know where I mean?"

"Yeah."

"If I'm not there by nightfall on the second day, you leave and you don't look back, understand?"

"Scarlett." He hugs me so tight it hurts but I don't want to let go. "Please come with me. Please just come away with me now."

I hear how his voice wavers but just shake my head again, unable to speak.

"Do you love him?" he asks.

I draw back and look up at my little brother. I nod my head. "I think I do."

"I'm glad." He tries for a smile and hugs me to him again, holding me tighter than he's ever held me before turning and disappearing into the tunnel.

I wipe my eyes as I make my way back up the stairs. It's the right thing to do. I know it. But I also realize, in a way, by saying out loud that I would be there in two days' time meant that it was a possibility I would not. And that this, tonight, was very possibly goodbye forever.

My mind is preoccupied as I reach the top of the stairs and turn the corner toward Cristiano's bedroom. I don't know where else to go when he's not here, in the house. I'm an imposter without him to validate my presence. I don't realize in time that the door is ajar or maybe I just don't remember having left it that way. But when I walk inside, I stop dead because the room is not empty.

And it's not Cristiano standing there.

It's Dante.

And he has the gun Cristiano gave me pointed right at me.

24

CRISTIANO

Blood. Me on the cold, white marble floor. No. Not cold. But dark. Slippery like that night. Slipping in my own blood.

Someone calls my name but it's an echo.

"David sends his regards."

My uncle did this. My uncle slaughtered my family. *Our* family.

"Your wife is a dirty whore."

Not a virgin.

"Your wife is a dirty whore. I may never have fucked her but let me tell you something. After seeing her take her Uncle Jacob's filthy dick, I really couldn't get it up for her anymore. That's some nasty shit."

No, not a virgin.

I punished her for it.

She paid for it.

"It won't hurt as much."

It was her uncle who'd hurt her. What had my father said?

"You're blood. Never forget that blood matters, boys."

Blood massacred my family.

Blood massacred hers. Blood violated her.

Our blood is corrupted.

Commotion around me. I open my eyes and see Marcus Rinaldi's face. His eyes are open, too. Looking at me. But they're empty. Dead. The knife still sticking out the side of his neck.

I reach for it. I want to dig it deeper. I need to. I want to sever his head from his body.

But as the room fades again, I realize I have what I wanted. The voices become echoes in the background. I have exactly what I asked for.

I know what Marcus said to my mother that horrified her.

I know that he's dead by my hand.

There wasn't anything else. I never planned for anything after this. I can let go. I can leave it. Leave the betrayal. Leave the constant pain of life.

Just go.

But then there's Scarlett.

25

SCARLETT

"Where were you?" Dante asks. "And where's your piece of shit brother?"

A soldier appears at the door. "Not up here," he says.

"Find the fucker."

"What's going on?" I ask.

He uncocks the gun and shifts his grip to look at it.

I exhale, touch my hand to my pocket, grateful my passport wasn't under the pillow. I look around to find Cerberus is gone.

"What's going on?" I ask again, wondering if he can hear the panic in my voice. "Where's Cristiano?"

He opens the chamber of the pistol and drops the bullets into the palm of his hand, pocketing them and tucking the gun into the back of his jeans before turning back to me. He studies me for a long minute, and it takes all I have to not back away when he closes the space between us.

"Where did you get the gun?"

"Cristiano gave it to me. Give it back."

He snorts. "Right." With the flat of his hand against my belly nudges me to the wall. "You're a liar, Scarlett De La Cruz. Just like the rest of your family." He stands just inches from me and I stare up into eyes just a few shades darker than Cristiano's. My heart is racing but I need to keep my face impassive, unreadable.

"I doubt your brother would like to hear how you put your hands on me."

His expression changes, something sad passing through his eyes before they harden again.

"Cristiano should have killed you on day one."

"Where is he?" I ask.

The pressure of his hand on my belly intensifies.

"Don't act innocent. That may have worked on my brother, but it won't work on me," he says, his jaw tight. He's stronger than me. And he wants to hurt me. I see it and I need to be careful with him. He shifts his grip to my arms squeezing hard enough that I know there will be bruises. "Where is your brother, Scarlett?" he spits my name.

"You're hurting me."

"Am I?" He spins me around, grips a handful of my hair and tugs it back so tightly I let out a cry. "How's this then? Better?"

I have one hand locked around his forearm but the way I'm twisted, it's no use. I can't budge him.

"I'm your brother's wife," I remind him. "Let me go!"

"He did what he had to do for the family. That's the only reason you're his wife. Don't read too much into him fucking you. You're a piece of ass. That is all you are. All you ever were." He takes my other arm and twists it behind my back. I don't think it'll take much to snap the bone. "Where's your brother? Where did you two disappear to?"

"You're going to break my arm." It hurts so much. "Please."

"How did you do it?" His voice breaks. "How did he get to him?"

My heart drops to my belly. Who got to him? "Dante." I turn my head as much as I can. "Please tell me where he is. Where's Cristiano?"

"I was starting to think I was wrong about you, you know that? I was starting to think maybe you really did care about my brother. That was my bad."

"I do care."

He spins me around and slams me so hard against the wall that my vision blurs. I have to grab hold of him to steady myself.

"I should kill you." He wraps his hand around my throat.

"Where is he?" I ask as he squeezes.

"Fuck my promise. It doesn't matter anymore anyway. I should kill you here and now."

"Where is he?" I manage, clawing at his forearm as his grip tightens.

He hauls me up by my throat, forcing me onto my tip toes as he dips his head lower so we're nose to nose.

"Where is he?" he asks, spitting the words.

My nails dig into his forearm but it's no use. I can't get enough air.

"He's dead, Scarlett. He's fucking dead."

SCARLETT

Dead?
 No.
 No.

Dante drops me and I hit the floor, my head bouncing off hard stone.

Cristiano is dead?

"Did you find those pieces of shit?" someone asks.

I roll onto my side gasping for breath, the back of my head throbbing.

"Just the girl."

I struggle to open my eyes and the room spins, the two of them standing over me like giants. Dante and David.

"She'll have to do."

I hear Cerberus's growl, turn my head just enough to see him stalk into the room, teeth bared.

"For fuck's sake. Get that beast away from me." It's David. Cristiano's uncle.

I watch Dante take Cerberus and walk him away from us, but when David reaches down to grab hold of my arm and roughly haul me up, Cerberus tries to lunge for him.

"Cerberus!" Dante tries to command him but even as my head lolls, I can see the effort it's taking him to hold the huge dog back.

David has me by both arms and gives me a hard shake. "Look at me."

I try. I can't seem to keep my head up or my eyes open, not to mention getting my legs under me without my knees giving out.

"Fuck," David curses.

"What do you want with her? We go after Felix now. Leave her in one of the cells. I'll take care of her when I'm finished with Felix," Dante says.

"That's not going to work for me."

"I made my brother a promise. Leave her to me."

"Your brother's dead. Any promises are void."

More men enter the room as I'm finally able to stand upright.

"I promised," Dante says. "Dead or alive."

David turns back to me, grasps my jaw with one hand and tilts my face up to look closely at me. He hands me off to one of the men who just entered.

"Cristiano," I croak, my throat hoarse after being nearly choked to death.

"Take her to the chopper."

"I said no!" Dante argues.

David goes to him. "Listen to me," he starts, voice menacing, but quickly shifting. David sighs, hangs his head. He looks back up at Dante who is a few inches taller than him. He smiles. "Your brother is dead, Dante. You and I are all that's left of the Grigori family. I love you like a son. You know that. I've taken care of you like a father when you family was murdered. When your brother couldn't be there for you."

"I know that."

"Let me take care of this one final loose end. Then we can get on with our lives."

Dante looks at him and I see how David's tone and words are getting to him. Either David is a very good actor or what he's saying is authentic. I'm going with the former.

"It's my final promise to my brother."

"Your brother was fooled by her. She deserves what I have planned."

"And what's that?"

"She'll get exactly what she deserves and Felix will never get his hands on her. He'll never use her to make the cartel fall in line and come after us."

Dante looks at me over his shoulder, but I can't read him at all. "No," he says to his uncle.

"What did you say?" David asks.

"I promised my brother," Dante says firmly.

David squares his shoulders. "Your brother is dead."

Dante glances at me once more, the look in his eyes one of utter pain, complete defeat. He nods.

"Get her on the chopper," David orders the soldiers.

CRISTIANO

Let go.

My mind fights the fog and each time it does, pain comes raging back, the sounds too loud, the lights too bright.

Let go.

I slip again. It's easier like this. Easier to slip away.

Crème caramel eyes.

Scarlett.

Pain.

If you die, she dies.

I know that. Her life is linked to mine. She will only survive if I survive.

The light changes. It's brighter and softer at once. And warm. It's warm here. A little girl's giggles bubble around the other noises. I open my eyes and look down at Elizabeth. She's so little. Maybe two.

We're at the beach. I buried her in the sand and I'm tickling her tiny feet. She's giggling and giggling and although she can pull away, she doesn't.

"Cristiano," my mother calls.

I turn to look over my shoulder at her. She's standing at the pier. And she's wearing the same dress she had on the night of the massacre. It's already stained red.

"Cristiano."

Giggles draw me back to my little sister who is wiggling her toes waiting for me to tickle her again.

If you die, she dies.

I close my eyes and feel the pain again. Hear the sounds blotting out everything else. Machines and people and too much noise.

Let go.

I'm so tired I want to let go but there's some part of me that won't let me do it.

"Cristiano."

This time when I look up, mom's closer. She's standing just a few feet away. So close I can smell her perfume. I had forgotten the scent along with everything else.

"Mom."

I stand up. I'm taller than her now. Does she know her throat is slit? Does she know the blood has dried around the gash?

I swallow, try not to look at it. It's dark behind her. Shadows all around her.

"I'm sorry," I tell her. "I'm sorry I couldn't stop him. I'm sorry I couldn't help you."

She smiles, reaches out a hand to touch my face. The way she used to when any of us fell or hurt ourselves when we were little. Her hand isn't warm like it used to be though. It's cold.

"It wasn't your fault."

That's when it happens. When it all comes flooding back. When all the memories I'd lost take me under like a tidal wave. Like a tsunami. I stand under the weight of them and look into my mother's eyes, trying not to see the gash on her throat as everything rushes me.

I stumble but she holds my hand and somehow, she steadies me.

The sun is gone. I didn't notice the clouds that rolled in, but I feel the wind, bitter and punishing.

I look down, seeing Elizabeth. She's not in the sand anymore. She's standing beside our mother holding her other hand. She's five now and she, too, is wearing the dress she wore the day she was killed. She too is cut, bleeding. No, not bleeding anymore. She already bled.

"I'm so sorry," I tell my little sister as an unbearable pain twists in my side.

Elizabeth reaches her other hand to me and holds mine.

"I miss you," I tell her, then turn to my mom. "I miss you all so much."

My mom reaches out to touch my face, wiping my cheek. Her finger is smeared with red when she pulls her hand away.

"I know you do but you can't stay," she says, and the scene shifts again, the clouds gone, the sun back. Elizabeth bright and happy again, no blood, just her pudgy little body in her bright yellow bumble bee bathing suit.

"Why not?" It would be so easy.

Elizabeth squeezes my hand and I look down to her. "You have to go back." It's like moving through mud here. Even shifting my gaze from one to the other is like dragging myself through thick mud.

"Why not?" I ask my mom again.

"Because she needs you. If you die, she dies," my mother says. "And you made her a promise."

Crème caramel eyes. Scarlett. Scarlett alone again. Scarlett unprotected again.

I promised to keep her safe and I'm breaking my promise.

Pain. Bright, fluorescent lights. Noise. So much fucking noise.

I blink, feel my mom's cool hand on my cheek again. I look at her, see her eyes again, fading now.

"Keep your promise," she says to me and then she's gone.

28

SCARLETT

The chopper lifts off. A soldier straps me in as we veer sharply west and I catch my breath, grasping hold of the edges of the seat.

I hate this chopper.

David is sitting across from me, facing me. In his eyes I see his hate.

Cristiano is dead.

I felt it, didn't I?

"How?" I ask him, my voice so small in the scream of the chopper's blades.

"Your lover killed him," David says.

"My...Marcus? He's not...Marcus killed him?"

"Don't pretend to care."

I'm not pretending but I don't bother to explain that. Cristiano is dead. He used up all nine of his lives.

The chopper dips low unexpectedly and I gasp, my stomach lurching before that brick settles in again.

Dead.

Gone.

I'll never see him again and all I can think is how much I'll miss him.

"I didn't betray him," I tell his uncle, not that it matters anymore. Not that he'll believe me.

He doesn't say anything, not for a long time and I'm not sure what I expect him to say. What I want him to say. But I have a feeling I won't feel the loss of Cristiano for too long. I have a feeling I won't have time to mourn him.

At least I got Noah out. If I'm not at the square in two days' time, he'll disappear. He'll know what happened to Cristiano. He'll figure out what happened to me and he'll know he has to disappear.

He'll be safe at least.

"Where are you taking me?" I ask David.

"Back to your people."

"I have no people."

"No, I guess you don't. But that only makes you more valuable to me."

"What do you mean?"

"Felix Pérez has a coup on his hands."

"Felix? What does he have to do with anything?"

"And he is the only one who can give me what I need now."

"What's that?"

"Sir," one of the soldiers wearing a headset interrupts us. "The jet is ready. Chopper lands in less than five minutes. We're cleared to take off as soon as everyone's on board. We'll have a ten-minute window, so we'll need to hurry."

David nods, stretches his neck to look out at whatever we're flying toward. I'm facing the wrong way so I can't see.

"Do they have what we need on board?"

"Yes, sir," the soldier says, eyes bouncing off me.

"You get the girl on the plane," he says, gaze still out the window. "If she fights you knock her out by any means necessary."

"What plane? Where the hell are you taking me?" I ask when David turns his attention back to me.

He doesn't answer me though and I shift my gaze to the window as we begin a hurried descent toward a long runway at what must be a small, private airport. If I crane my neck, I can see the jet that's parked on the runway, one man standing outside looking up at the chopper, two more soldiers hovering around the stairs that lead into the plane. I see that one is smoking as we near the ground.

I scan the expanse of the fenced-in airport with all its open space. Beyond that is a sparsely populated neighborhood.

The chopper touches down, the landing bumpy.

David opens the door and slides out, casually adjusting his jacket sleeve as he walks toward the waiting jet.

"Let's go," his soldier says to me.

I turn to him, note the pistol in its shoulder holster. He's in gear like Cristiano and his men when he first came to that tower and stole me. He was ready for war then. This man, he's ready for war now. And the most dangerous one is standing outside the waiting jet.

I unbuckle the belt, work my arms out of it. The soldier steps out of the chopper. The other one is waiting for me to exit first. As I duck down, the one outside grabs hold of my arm, his grip hard. A warning.

"I'm Cristiano's wife," I remind him. "He wouldn't want you handling me like this."

He looks at me for a long moment. I'm pretty sure I've never seen him at the house. Not that I remember all the soldiers, but this one scares me. Inside his eyes, I see a great expanse of emptiness.

"Let's go," he says, and I walk with him toward the waiting plane. The chopper blades blow my hair around my face as we pass David and the other men who simply watch as I'm loaded onto the plane.

That's when I resist. I can't not. I feel like if I get on that plane, there won't be any going back. My fate will be sealed.

But it's no use resisting. There are at least six of

them and one of me. Not to mention that most of them are armed. Once we're on the plane and he deposits me into a seat, I stop fighting. He straps my belt and takes the seat beside me as David and the other soldiers climb on board. Then the cabin door is closed.

My heart races when David takes the seat across from mine. Someone hands him a rectangular box. He thanks them, then shifts his gaze out the window.

"Tell me what's happening," I say as the jet begins to speed down the runway. I feel the moment we lift off, hear the sound of the wheels folding into the belly of the plane. "Please," I add, eyeing that box on his lap.

He turns back to me after checking the time on his watch.

"I'm selling you to Felix," he says flatly.

"What? You told Dante—"

"You'd rather I put a bullet in your head now?"

I quiet.

"Didn't think so. Besides, that'd be a waste. Those loyal to your father have rebelled against him taking over the cartel, while you and your brother are still alive. Still out there."

I swallow at the mention of Noah.

"Don't worry, I don't care if your brother somehow managed to slip away. Although I am curious how."

"What do you mean about those who are rebelling?"

"Felix is a smart guy I have to admit. He'll make an example out of you. Show those still stubbornly loyal to your father what happens when you cross him."

I stare at him.

"Don't you want to know how?"

"I don't care what he does to me."

"You might care after you figure it out."

I don't say anything.

"You know what?" he asks, leaning toward me a little. "I just want to see your face when I tell you. And since I don't plan on sticking around for the main event, well, I don't really care about the surprise factor."

"I'm Cristiano's wife. You can't treat me like this."

"My nephew's dead. Or if he's not yet, he will be soon."

"What?"

He shrugs his shoulder dismissively. "There's an auction tomorrow night. The big one buyers have come from all over the world for. He already sold his one special item up for bid but now there is a second."

"What the hell are you talking about?"

"The virgin daughter of one of the once most powerful men of the Italian mafia families. Almost grown up. Fifteen is a good age. Some men like them young. I hear your uncle did."

I suddenly know exactly who he's talking about and I feel sick.

"I personally don't understand the draw, but I have to admit it brings in good money."

"Cristiano's sister is dead."

"Yes, she is, because you can't trust a fucking cartel idiot soldier to do the job right."

"Mara?"

"She goes by Lizzie now. It's easier for everyone. No harm, no foul."

"She's alive. And you've known it all this time?"

He smiles, shakes his head. "That's not the part you should worry about, Scarlett. Didn't you hear what I said?" he pauses for effect. "There's now a second special item to bid on. Can you guess what—or I should say *who*—that is?"

I try not to react. Not to show any emotion at all even though my heart is beating so fast I swear it's trying to bulldoze its way out of my chest.

"Just think of those cousins and nieces and nephews hearing about how Felix Pérez stripped the cartel princess naked and put her on an auction block to be sold like a piece of meat to any number of Cristiano Grigori's enemies. And let me tell you, there are plenty. My nephew wasn't exactly good at making friends."

"Do you even care about him at all? Do you care that he's dead?"

"Of course, I do. He's my brother's son. I'm not a beast, Scarlett. But again, you digress."

He opens the box on his lap then and I see a syringe lying inside. I drag my gaze from it back up to his.

"I'll just leave you with one thought before I give you the gift of sleep."

He lifts the syringe out of the box, takes the cap off and drops it onto the floor. He gestures to the soldier beside me to stretch my arm out, shoving my sleeve up and gripping it with two hands so hard, it burns.

"Don't," I try but it doesn't matter, does it? Cristiano is dead and if he's not, he will be soon. It's what he said and why would he lie? And with what he and Felix have in store for me, isn't it better if I'm knocked out?

"Just imagine," he starts, leaning in close. Pushing the air out of the barrel, a few drops of liquid fall on my bare arm before I feel the point puncture skin. "How many men will be bidding to have you. The things they'll do to you. Hell, if he's really smart, if he really wants to make that example hit home, maybe he'll just have them line up and take turns. Just think about that."

My head lolls back. It's hard to keep my eyes

open or focused as he pulls the needle out and puts it back in its box.

"Noah," I say, unable to lift my arms or hands or legs when the soldier releases me.

"Noah will have it easy in comparison. He'll have a price on his head for the rest of his life which I'm going to guess will be a short one."

"Go to hell," I manage just before I can't open my eyes anymore.

"I expect you'll be there sooner than me. Good night, Scarlett De La Cruz. Sleep tight."

29

CRISTIANO

Loud voices cut through the nothingness of a heavy sleep. A familiar sleep. One I don't want.

"Let me through." I recognize this one. The others I don't know. All men and one woman. She's the reasonable one.

"For fuck's sake if you don't get out of my way, I'm going to kill every one of you mother fuckers."

Dante. I try to make my face work but something's wrong. I want to tell them to let him in. But let him in where? And why can't I fucking move? Why can't I wake up?

"He's being moved from your facility," another familiar voice says. Charlie. Yes, Charlie. He's also reasonable. Calm.

"Get security up here," the woman's voice says.

There's a crash and then the voices are louder.

"Shit." Dante again.

I should open my eyes. I'm trying to.

"Cris." It's Dante and he's closer now. "Fuck. Cris. Fuck. Open your eyes, man."

Someone pulls up an eyelid and shines a bright light into my eye. I groan against the intrusion. At least I can groan. Make some sound of resistance.

"He's heavily sedated. Help me. Take that."

I feel my arm lifted then set back down before someone prods my side. Now that fucking hurts.

"There's no reason for him to be sedated. Surgery was over a full twenty-four hours ago." The last part fades out as I start to drift off again. Maybe I can go back to that beach. See Elizabeth and mom one more time. What had they said last time?

"Wake up, Brother," Dante says and in usual form, he slaps my face a couple of times. "You need to open your eyes. I need you to open your fucking eyes."

"Let's get him on that stretcher. Dante, you take that side." It's Dr. Marino.

The instant I'm lifted pain cuts through my side. That groan must be me because the doctor's yelling at them to be careful.

"Can't you give him something to wake him up?" Dante snaps, his tone urgent. He's closer to my ear now and I'm being rolled. I hear Charlie again and the woman. They're arguing. Charlie will win.

"It won't be safe," Dr. Marino says.

I hear a ding. An elevator. The wheels bump as they cross the threshold and I feel my side again. My head lolls and I open my eyes, or I think I do, and I see Marcus Rinaldi. I see his dead eyes. See the knife in his throat.

I put it there. I killed him.

The doors swoosh open and we're rolling again. A few minutes later, we're outside. I feel it in the change of temperature, in the fresh, not chemically scented air.

"Is he answering?" Dante asks someone.

"Nothing yet. Calls are going right to voice mail. He must have his phone off."

"Charlie," Dante says as I'm loaded into something. Whoever is lifting the stretcher is not careful but I'm drifting again. "Do you have my uncle's private number? My phone is dead, and I don't remember it."

A sense of dread washes over me. Why is he trying to call him? He shouldn't. I need to warn him but I'm not sure why.

"We'll wait to call him when Cristiano is awake and alert," Charlie says.

"Fuck that. Fuck. He needs to know he's alive. Fuck!"

"It can wait. He can wait."

"No, he can't."

"What's the urgency, Dante?'"

That dread is back.

"David sends his regards."

I swallow. Even that fucking hurts. "No." It comes out a groan as I fight whatever has me in this sleep state.

"Cris?" Dante asks. We're in a moving vehicle. I feel that much. "Come on, man. I thought you were fucking dead. Please wake the fuck up!"

"Dante. Take it easy," the doctor says. "He'll wake up soon. I gave him something to hurry it along as much as I safely can."

"How long?" Dante asks.

"Couple of hours."

"We may not have a couple of hours."

"We'll get him to the island. To his own bed. Scarlett being there will help," Charlie says.

Scarlett.

"If you die, she dies."

I feel my hands fist at least a little. It feels like that time I heard Lenore and David talking. I was waking up. It was a memory. I know now. I'm sure.

Betrayed. He betrayed me twice. But why did he let me live? Why not kill me, too? Why not kill Dante and me both?

"She's not there," my brother says, his tone more quiet.

"What do you mean she's not there?" Charlie asks.

The vehicle takes a turn. I swear I feel every

fucking thing in my side where Rinaldi managed to stab me before I killed him.

"Dante?" It's Charlie again.

"David took her. We thought he was dead. Someone told him Rinaldi had killed Cristiano and he took her."

David has Scarlett?

"Took her where?" Charlie asks.

"Fuck." Silence. Weighted silence I can feel. "I don't know."

Something begins to beep frantically, and I feel hands on me, the doctor telling Dante and Charlie to back off.

"He said he knew exactly what to do with her," Dante says so quietly that I almost don't hear.

"You let him take your brother's wife?"

"I thought...he told me Cris was dead! I thought she'd betrayed him. Tipped off Rinaldi. I thought...Fuck!"

30

SCARLETT

I blink my eyes open, looking up at the ceiling of a dimly lit, small room. It takes me a moment to remember what happened. To remember that Cristiano is dead. And that his brother handed me off to David who will now sell me back to the cartel.

This is my punishment because they think I betrayed Cristiano.

Not that either of them would have let me live, even if I could have convinced them that I hadn't. They hate me because I am a De La Cruz.

At least Noah is safe. But is he? How long has it been? Is he still in Naples waiting for me to come?

I turn my head to look around the room. I'm alone but there's a camera set up directly across from the bed. The red light is blinking. I'm either being recorded or someone's watching me now.

There's a chair in the far corner and two doors, both closed. The wooden doors are old, splintering. This whole place feels forgotten. A red neon light blinks outside from a street sign. The ratty yellowed lace curtain, only half-hanging off the rod, barely filters the red light as raindrops tap softly on the glass.

I try to pull my arm in, but I can't. I look up to find my right wrist is handcuffed to the bed.

At least I'm not naked. That's something, right?

"Hell, if he's really smart, if he really wants to make that example hit home, maybe he'll just have the men line up and take turns. Just think about that."

My eyes fall on that camera again.

Maybe he already sold me. Maybe Felix has me here awaiting my fate, the camera ready to record every minute of my degradation. Ready to broadcast for anyone who misses the live show.

I shudder, sit up, drawing my knees in toward my body. It's cold in the room. My arm hurts where he gave me the shot and a tiny bruise has formed. But that's the least of my problems.

This can't be about me anymore. I'm dead, I know that. The only thing standing between me and death was Cristiano and he's gone. I can't think about that now. I can't think about the loss of him.

At least I got Noah out, I tell myself again. Turning my face away from the camera so they don't see the few tears slip out before I can stop them.

What had David said? There's an auction.

Is it the same auction that boat of women was heading to? Women and girls. And Lenore's granddaughter, Mara is there. If David is telling the truth, that is. Why wouldn't he, though? Why would he lie about that? There's no reason to lie to me about it.

But he knew about Mara all along and never told Cristiano or Dante or even Lenore? He knew she was alive?

No. It's worse than that. He'd planned it. They'd just screwed up and taken the wrong little girl.

He'd planned for Elizabeth to be kidnapped. Cristiano's little sister. His niece. Which means he was involved in their massacre.

Why?

I drop my head, shake it. The why doesn't matter, not anymore. Did Cristiano find out at least? Before he died? No. He couldn't have.

I steel myself and raise my head. No time to mourn. I look straight at the camera. Straight at the cowards on the other side of it.

I can die quietly. Or I can try to do something to help Mara. To help those women. To avenge Cristiano at least a little.

So, I settle into my seat. I look straight into that lens and I plot, raising my middle finger at whoever is watching.

Because I'll fight.

Because I've never been the quiet type.

CRISTIANO

I don't know how long I fight for. All I know is every time I regain a modicum of consciousness, I'm right back where I was when I heard Dante. Charlie. Right back to fighting this fog.

David has Scarlett.

Those are the three words that repeat in my head every time I feel the weight of life. Of waking. That and dread. Dread for her.

Something cold and wet touches the back of my hand. I turn my head toward whatever it is even though I can't yet open my eyes. That cold and wet turns warm and soft and I realize it's Cerberus. He's nuzzling his head into my hand.

I feel myself smile just a little. This one comfort. I move my fingers as much as I can, and he must feel it because I hear him whine then let out a small bark.

"Cristiano?"

Keeping my hand cupped around Cerberus's head, I draw my other arm up. It feels like I'm dragging it through mud.

"Fuck," Dante mutters, but I hear his relief.

I touch my face, my head. And somehow, I force my eyelids to open. I see my brother peering down at me, his hair a mess like he's been running his hands through it for hours. Shadows darken the skin beneath his eyes. He hasn't slept.

"How much time?" I ask as I try to push myself up to a seat. It's fucking impossible. My side hurts like a mother fucker. I push through it and Dante adjusts the pillow then hands me a glass of water.

"Three nights since you killed Rinaldi."

"He's dead." It's a fact. I don't need confirmation. I will never forget his eyes. I won't forget the feel of the knife cutting into his throat.

"Yeah. He's dead," Dante confirms anyway.

I take a sip of the water then push it away. I look at Cerberus who is half sitting by the bed, tail wagging behind him as he nuzzles his nose into the palm of my hand. I pet him but turn to my brother.

"Scarlett," I say.

He runs his hands through his hair again. Turns away momentarily. "He stabbed you where you'd been shot. It's why it's so bad."

"Scarlett." I think about how she calls me a Neanderthal. I sound like one.

Dante turns back to me, expression dark. "Gone."

"Of her own free will?" I'm not sure why I ask. I know the answer.

He shakes his head. "David took her."

"And you let him?"

He has the decency to look down. "Charlie told me what he thinks about David. But it can't be true, Cris. He wouldn't do anything against us."

I push the blanket off. The pain when I swing my legs off the bed causes the room to go black for a minute.

"You're in no shape—"

"It was him," I cut Dante off, shove his hand away and grip the edge of the nightstand. "It was him who ordered it."

"Ordered what?"

I stand. Stop again. Wait for the room to stop spinning. I press my hand to my side. It feels hot but a glance down confirms it's not bleeding.

"Ordered what?" Dante asks again this time through gritted teeth. Because he's got to have put some things together too if Charlie talked to him.

I look at my brother. I swear there's more gray around his temples. Fuck. He's only twenty-six.

"He was behind it. He ordered it. He murdered our family."

Dante's eyes betray his emotion, betray what he

knows deep down, but he closes them, shakes his head. "No, Brother. Rinaldi lied to you."'

"He knew that bastard had—" I stop. Dante doesn't know about the rape. I hadn't realized my uncle knew and he'd been so smooth in covering up how when I'd questioned him.

"No, Cristiano."

I walk to my closet, pull on the first pair of jeans I see along with a T-shirt. It hurts like fucking hell when I raise my arm to do it. I pull on socks and a pair of boots.

"Where did he take Scarlett?" I ask him when I'm back in the bedroom and open the drawer where I keep one of the Glocks. I slip the holstered weapon onto my shoulder before pulling on a jacket.

"Where the fuck do you think you're going?" my brother asks.

"I'm going to get my wife." I change direction, head toward him. "Where did he take her?"

He doesn't back away. "You can't go anywhere. You need to heal."

I get in his face. "You let him take my wife."

"She betrayed you!"

"She did not! And I told you that you don't lay a fucking finger on her, not if I'm alive and not if I'm dead. You knew that. You promised me you'd protect her. You fucking promised me."

He doesn't back down, not at first. But then steps back, drops to a seat on the chair and wraps one hand around the back of his neck before shifting his gaze out the window.

There's a knock on the door then and Antonio opens it, the expression on his face urgent.

He stops just inside the door when he sees us.

"Cristiano," he starts, looking me over. "Are you—"

"I'm fine."

"I have a location in Rotterdam."

"Fuck," Dante says.

I only glance at him. I'm so pissed at him I could kill him.

"Is my wife there?"

"There's some buzz that would suggest she is or will be soon."

"And my uncle. Where exactly is he?"

"The plane he took landed at a private airfield outside of Rotterdam three nights ago," Dante answers.

We both turn to him. "I had it tracked."

"Why?" I ask. "Why would you do that if you don't believe he'd betray us?"

"I don't fucking know." Dante shakes his head, runs his hand through his messy hair yet again.

"You do fucking know."

"He's always done right by me. By us."

"No, Brother. He hasn't. And he owes me some answers." I turn to Antonio. "Have you arranged transportation?"

He nods once.

"And Noah? Any sign?"

"Tunnel was accessed recently," Antonio says. I told him where to look. "The vehicle you mentioned on the other side gone."

"Good."

"You want me to put men out looking for him?"

"No. Better if the kid disappears."

"All right."

"Let's go."

"I'm coming with you," Dante says.

I stop, look back at him. "Why?"

"Because if you're right then Uncle David owes me answers too."

"Fine. But if you get in my way, I'll fucking hurt you, brother or not."

"Understood."

Antonio walks out first and just before I step away, Dante puts a hand on my arm. "I'm sorry. I just thought...I thought I'd lost you again."

I pull my arm away. "You can apologize to my wife when we get her back and we'd better get her back. Alive."

32

SCARLETT

A woman brings me food and water. Each time she keeps her eyes cast down and is let inside by a different man. He stands at the door with his hand on the key in the lock as she clears out one dish to swap it out for another.

I eat a little bit of the stale bread but leave the cold meat. The scent of which makes my stomach turn. It looks to be leftovers someone else didn't finish. I drink all the water, which I'm grateful is bottled.

I realize the bucket beside the bed is my toilet. My cuffed arm just allows me access to it and when I have to pee, I try not to think of the camera.

I've spent two nights here, I guess, assuming that I was knocked out only for a few hours. When I woke up it was already dark. I can hear noise on the street if I concentrate. I think we're in a city, but this house or at least my room is up high enough and must be tucked out of the way enough, that I have to strain my ears to hear it.

It's the morning of the third day that I hear different voices.

David's is one. He's speaking English. The other one I recognize too. I heard it the morning Jacob kidnapped me and took me to that pier.

"Cover her for fuck's sake."

I shudder at the memory of Jacob's blood splattering across my face and remember the scent of the jacket that someone had draped over my shoulders. The door opens just as I place the voice.

Felix Pérez stands in the doorway of the decrepit room. He finishes what he was saying, a smile easy on his face when he takes in first the surroundings and then me.

He steps inside and David follows.

Felix looks different than I remember him, but it's been so many years. He's still as short, just a little over five and a half feet. And he's losing his hair. I notice when he walks inside, glancing at my bucket before crossing the room to look out of the window, that a bald spot has begun to form at the crown of his head. I wonder if he realizes it. Do men realize when they start to go bald? I mean, it's not like they see that part of their head.

He has his jacket draped over his shoulders. His suit is a worn-out beige, the style about a decade old.

It looks like a knock off. Like him. An imposter in a stolen role. He's also grown softer around the middle. I notice the paunch when he turns back to face me.

So different from Cristiano in every way.

Cristiano.

My heart sinks a little deeper at the thought of him. He's gone. I'll never see him again.

"You were at the dock," I say.

He nods.

"Did you have Jacob killed?"

"Do you miss him? I thought you'd be grateful."

"You ordered it."

"I didn't need both him and Marcus. Marcus was more useful at the time," he says, glancing at David with a sly grin, making me wonder what that exchange is about.

"Are you hurt, Cousin?" Felix asks.

His question causes my focus back to him and he's cocked his head to look at my face. He has his hands in his pockets. A heavy watch and gold chains crowd both wrists. I remember how much he liked to show off anything gold. Remember how my dad found it so distasteful, found Felix distasteful, like Jacob. The one comment that still comes to mind was about how real men didn't need to prove themselves with displays of wealth or status. That only those who didn't belong needed so hard to fit in.

"I don't know that we're technically cousins," I say. Probably not the smartest thing to say.

"By marriage." He shrugs a shoulder. "I thought you might appreciate having family in your time of need."

"Are you demented?"

He smiles. "You are ungrateful." His accent is strong.

David clears his throat. "We good?" he asks.

Felix shifts his gaze to David only momentarily. "Are you hurt, Cousin?" he asks as he comes closer.

Without waiting for my reply, he takes my jaw in one hand and tilts my face up to his before brushing hair back from my forehead.

"Some bruising," he comments. "It'll take the price down, of course. Damaged goods."

I tug my face out of his hands. "Don't touch me."

He grins, grips my jaw again, tighter this time. "Does she have all her teeth?" he asks and gestures to David with a nod of his head. David takes hold of both sides of my head while Felix pries my mouth open. I'd bite off his fingers if I could, but I can't at the angle they're holding me.

He makes a satisfied sound.

"Not a virgin though," he says, still peering inside my mouth like I'm some animal. "Virgins bring in more money."

"That's on your father-in-law," David says. "Nothing I can do about that."

"Sick man," Felix comments casually. Did everyone know what *Uncle* Jacob had done to me? Did they just stand back and let it happen?

"Anal virgin?" he asks, releasing my mouth, pulling his fingers away before my teeth snap shut.

I tug at my bound arm but of course it's no use so I draw my head back as he starts to discuss the possibilities of selling that particular part of my anatomy, and spit in his face.

He stops talking, that smug grin instantly wiped away.

My heart races even as I try for a victorious smile.

David mutters a curse. Felix first uses the back of his hand to wipe off my spit on his right cheekbone, then backhands me so hard with that same hand that I fall back on the bed. My head crashes against the wall, then the metal railing, the blow stunning me.

I feel the warmth of blood rolling down my cheek.

He straightens, adjusts his jacket over his shoulder, his expression of rage morphing back into a false smile. For a single instant I see the real Felix Pérez. And it terrifies me.

"Apologize!" David orders me.

Felix raises a hand. "No need," he says. "I expect no less from a De La Cruz. They're animals. I'd pour the contents of that bucket over your head but then

I'd have to smell you." He checks his watch. "Speaking of, we're on a tight schedule."

"We have a deal?" David asks.

"What deal?" I ask.

They both ignore me. Felix punches some numbers into his phone and turns it around to show David, who nods.

Felix calls to one of the men at the door, the one with the keys. He undoes my cuff from the rung of the headboard and re-cuffs my arms behind my back. He lifts me to stand, almost making me knock the bucket over as I do.

"Where are we going?" I ask Felix or David or anyone who will answer. I'm marched out of the room, noticing the apartment we're in, where two more men sit in the kitchen eating hamburgers. The TV playing in the background is in a language I don't understand. Sounds like German.

I'm taken down the stairs, the man simply dragging me along when I trip or don't move fast enough, before we're outside.

It's noisy beyond the alley where an SUV is waiting. It blocks my view of the street, of the people walking and the cars driving by, oblivious to what's happening here in this dark corner of their world.

The windows of the SUV are tinted an opaque black. I can't even make out how many people are inside.

I'm barefoot. I hadn't really thought about it

when I'd been in that room but the puddles of water on the street chill me as one of the doors is opened. I'm lifted up and placed in the back seat.

Felix climbs into the passenger seat and turns around as I'm strapped in by a woman who looks a lot like the one Marcus employed to prepare me for our wedding. She's sitting between me and one other passenger. A girl.

He glances at me, then over to her. "I'm sorry she smells, sweetheart. She wasn't bathed, I'm sure. You know those thugs."

I look at the girl in the shadowy car, the red lights blinking illuminating her only momentarily. She has long blonde hair, I see that. And huge crystal blue eyes. She leans around the woman to peer at me but doesn't speak and her expression doesn't change. Just huge, frightened eyes on me.

"She doesn't smell so bad," the girl says flatly, her accent American.

"You're too sweet, my little doll," Felix says, reaching his arm back to caress her face.

She shrinks back a little, but one cluck of his tongue and she leans her face into his hand. She's young. I see it now when the light from the street shines on her face. Fifteen or sixteen maybe and small.

I want to slap his hand away. I want to make him stop touching her.

"I'll miss you," he says to her.

She turns her head to look out the window.

"What do you say, Lizzie?" he asks.

Lizzie?

I peer more closely.

She turns back to him, same huge eyes a little shinier in the light. "I'll miss you too," she whispers but inside that whisper, I hear a hint of steel. Just a hint.

Felix smiles then as quickly as he'd struck me, he shifts his grip to twist a fistful of her hair painfully pulling her toward him.

The girl makes a sound but nothing else.

"Again," he commands.

"I'll miss you too, Felix. Very much." No steel this time. It's melted away. I guess ten years will do that to you.

"Good girl," he says, releasing her.

She looks down at her fisted hands in her lap. The woman between us unhooks something from her belt, unravels it. It's a leather strap, about six inches long. She raises it, crashes it down over the girl's hands.

I gasp, shocked.

The girl makes a sound but catches herself, swallows it down and releases her fists, laying them flat on her lap. I watch the angry red line form across the tops.

"Better," the woman says.

The girl remains silent, but I catch how her eyes

shift to mine momentarily. She must be afraid to get caught. They've trained her.

Felix looks at me. He gives me a grin. "Get comfortable. We've got a long ride." He turns back in his seat and switches on the radio to a station playing Spanish music.

33

CRISTIANO

The private jet lands in Rotterdam a few hours later. The flight was tense, to say the least, my brother quiet. He knows he did wrong. But I can't forgive him. Not yet.

Two cars wait for us at the airfield. Antonio, Dante and I climb into one, Dante sitting in the passenger seat.

"House is in the city. About thirty kilometers from here."

"You've got eyes on it?"

Antonio nods. "Only for the last couple of hours though. There are definitely two men inside and a woman."

"Scarlett?"

"Not sure yet."

I shift my gaze out the window.

"We'll find her, Cristiano," he says.

I watch passing cars as we merge into traffic.

She got Noah out. I'm glad she got him out. But she should have gone with him. Why didn't she? Was she waiting for me to return?

"Does she think I'm dead?" I ask. Antonio knows I'm talking to my brother.

There's a long silence. "I told her you were because I thought you were," he pauses, turns in his seat. I see him in my periphery. "She was upset to hear it."

I don't let myself feel anything at that. I can't. I need to focus now. The stakes are too high for emotion. For weakness.

"And my uncle?" I ask, only turning back to Antonio when I've schooled my features.

He's typing something into his phone. Antonio has contacts everywhere. And throughout this, I've learned that I can trust and rely on him.

"I'm just following up on a lead. He was at the house too, we know that."

"We need to get Scarlett back first. I'll deal with him after."

The rest of the drive is silent, and I watch the busy streets of the city as the driver weaves his way through dense traffic to a seedier looking part of town.

"There are three possible entry and exit points. Front door, side and back door. Downstairs windows are boarded up. The side door leads into an alley. The street itself is fairly busy so we'll have to keep a low profile. No busting in doors and no gunfire if we can help it. Not on street level at least. We've got half a dozen men in place. Your uncle used the side door to go in and out. We'll use that one too."

"I'll go in first," Dante says as the driver parks the car a block away and we climb out. He checks his weapon before tucking it out of sight.

"You'll stay with me," I tell him.

"This is my fault. I owe—"

"You'll stay with me or you'll stay in the car."

"You know I'm not a kid anymore."

"With me or in the car. Decide."

"Fine."

We walk down the street weaving into the crowds. When Antonio points out the house, I look up at it, at the dimly lit rooms upstairs, at the attic window. Rain drizzles overhead, steady and cold. Someone moves behind one of the windows, a shadow crossing the room.

I nod to Antonio and we move. I catch sight of our men as we near the alley where someone stands taking a piss against the dumpster. He's humming and when he sees us, he looks up. His smile vanishes instantly. Even stinking of alcohol, he must sense danger. He hurries to put his dick back in his pants and stumbles away.

Once he's gone, we head in. I take my pistol in

hand and make my way to the side door. Maybe being a little less careful than I should but feeling anxious.

If Scarlett's in this place, I need to get to her. Get her out.

The door is locked, as expected. Antonio touches my arm as he twists a silencer onto his weapon before he shoots out the lock. It's not as silent as I'd like but given the noise in the street, I'm hoping we'll still have the element of surprise.

I step in first followed by Antonio and Dante. The house must have been split into apartments at some point because the door we just broke in through opens up to a staircase and some storage areas. It's unused though, cobwebs and junk piled in every corner.

No welcome party. That's good. Unless they're waiting to ambush us upstairs.

I take the lead up the old wooden stairs which creak beneath our boots and hear the sound of a television coming from behind the closed door. The volume's turned pretty high. This could be good for us or bad for us, but we won't know until it's too late.

Here too, junk and forgotten furniture take up parts of the hallway. Antonio slips around me and walks to the second door which stands open. He gives the signal that it's clear.

I turn to my brother who moves into position on the opposite side of the door. "Ready?" I mouth.

He nods.

Without another moment's hesitation, I kick the door in, the wood splintering as it crashes against the far wall.

A woman screams and men curse, the tv still going in the background as a table is knocked over and weapons are drawn, the men clearly surprised.

I know in that moment Scarlett isn't here. Maybe she was at one point, but she's gone.

I know it as a gun battle breaks out. So much for no gunfire. I know it as the tv is shot out, as the woman dives to the kitchen floor, as the men take bullets that knock them back and down.

I know it when all the sound that's left in the place is that of our breathing, of the TV short-circuiting, of the woman whimpering on the kitchen floor.

"We'll need to move fast," Antonio says as I make my way down the hallway to check the rooms. I find them empty although there were people here at some point. Handcuffs hang from the headboards of the beds and the stench of fear clings to the walls.

"Upstairs," Dante says.

I turn back to find him holding the woman who is pointing up. I move, weapon ready, hurrying up the narrow, winding stairs to the attic room. Its door is left open, the bed empty, no handcuffs on this one. Just a bucket, a camera with its red light still blinking and one of Scarlett's shoes. Those ballet flats.

"She was here," I say, tucking my gun away and picking up the shoe. It's so small. She's so small. And on her own. No match for the men of our world.

Antonio and Dante walk in behind me as I push a few buttons on the camera to play back the recording. I see her then. Scarlett carried in. Unconscious. Dumped unceremoniously on the bed. Handcuffed to it. My uncle giving the orders from the sideline obvious even though there is no sound.

Dante stands beside me as we watch Scarlett wake. As I see her take in the surroundings. As I see her decide she'll fight even if it's impossible.

And when she gives the camera the finger, I give a half-hearted, bitter smile. "That's my girl."

"She's tough," Dante says, and I realize I said that out loud.

I push the button to forward through the footage until I get to Felix Pérez walking into the room. I watch them have a conversation. I watch her spit in his face. I watch him slap hers so hard he almost knocks her out. When she opens her eyes, she's dazed. She rights herself and I see the cut on her cheekbone, see blood stain her face.

That's the breaking point for me.

I close my hand over the screen, my throat tight, jaw tense, everything inside me wanting to break. To kill. To demolish.

I take the camera and smash it against the far wall the way I will smash both my uncle and Felix Pérez.

34

SCARLETT

We drive out of the city, mostly taking backroads to wherever we're going. The three of us in the backseat are quiet while Felix alternates between taking calls and singing along with the radio, like we're on some bazaar family road trip. It must be at least two hours later that we reach our destination, a hulking house in the middle of nowhere, guarded heavily at the gates and beyond.

There must be two dozen cars parked out front and that many more soldiers loitering around the vehicles.

"This is the end of the line, ladies," Felix says as the car pulls to a stop around back.

The girl, no, not the girl. I know her name. Her real name. *Mara* looks both curiously and fearfully up at the house.

Felix focuses his attention on me. "That's turned ugly. Don't make me hit you again."

The doors open and we're escorted out. Mara isn't handcuffed and she walks a few steps behind the woman, a soldier at her heels.

My soldier takes me by the arm and keeps shoving me toward the back door which is opened before we get to the stairs that lead up to it.

"This way," someone says, ushering us inside. "Two?" she asks Felix when she sees us. "I was expecting one."

"Change of plans. I'm sure you can accommodate us."

"Of course."

"Put them together. That one is a sly one," he tells her, pointing to me. "Keep your best guards on her." He turns to the woman who strapped Mara's hands in the SUV. "She needs to be bathed. Badly."

"Asshole," I can't help but mutter.

The woman raises her eyebrows and gives me a look.

Felix glances at me. "One more word and I'll cut out your tongue."

I keep my mouth shut.

"Shall I take care of it, sir?" the woman we drove with asks.

"Do. Without leaving marks."

She nods.

He turns to me. "She's got a talent for not leaving marks. Isn't that right, Lizzie?"

Lizzie—Mara—doesn't answer.

He shifts his attention back to the woman who let us in. I wonder to myself how women work with men like this, knowing what they're doing. Selling other women and girls.

"And this one, well, I don't need to tell you what will happen if this one isn't delivered in pristine condition. No one lays a finger on her. Helga will remain with her at all times."

"Yes, sir."

"Is he here?" I hear Felix ask as we're ushered upstairs by Helga.

"Not yet but we've had word his envoy is on its way."

I momentarily hear a harp as a server pushes a door open carrying an empty tray into the large kitchen. He doesn't spare us a glance as we're led up two flights of stairs to a luxurious hallway with gold and pink wallpaper and plush carpet. The patterns are dizzying. There are a dozen doors on this floor. As we walk past them, I hear some sound, but not a lot. What I can hear reminds me of the boat with those women. This must be the auction. This must be where they were brought.

Mara and I are taken to the room at the far end of the corridor. It's a bedroom more luxurious than any I've seen. The huge bed is the centerpiece, the fabric draping it like something out of a princess movie. Pink all around, as far as the eye can see. I wonder if a five-year-old decorated this place.

Three men accompany us inside and Helga starts right away.

"You, sit." She points to a chair in the far corner as if Mara is a dog.

Mara spares me a glance before walking to the chair and taking a seat.

Helga turns to me, looks me over, eyes scornful. I can't tell how old she is. She could be thirty or sixty with her gray-streaked hair drawn back into a tight bun, face pudgy, the lipstick she has on strangely out of place, too pink, too smudged. She's sturdy, built big.

She unhooks the same strap she'd used to strike Mara from her belt.

"Strip her. Get her on the bed on her back."

The men obey without a word, my struggles not hindering their efforts in the least, my curses doing nothing but earning a clucking of the tongue from Helga.

Once I'm naked, I'm lifted and hauled to the bed, my arms still behind my back, wrists still bound. The metal of the handcuffs digs into my lower back.

"Open her legs and keep her down."

"No!" Again, it's useless to fight. I know it. There are too many of them and I'm bound. One of the men takes hold of my shoulders to pin me to the bed. The others move to either side of me each taking a leg, spreading me wide.

Helga's gaze shifts to my exposed sex then to my eyes. "Wider." She runs the strap through the palm of her left hand, and I realize what she means to do. She'll strap me there. It'll leave a mark, won't it?

"Good," she says once my legs are at the point they'd break if they were spread any wider. "Hold her still."

She shifts her position slightly, I guess to get at me at a better angle, raises her arm and brings the strap down over my sex.

For a split second, all I hear is the sound of the strap, then nothing. Just nothing. And then the white-hot pain.

"You're a fucking sadist!" I shout when I can speak again.

She straps me again, not bothering to comment as she lashes me six more times. My crotch is on fire and I'm wriggling to get out of the way but can't. She's precise. She's done this before.

"It's enough," Mara says from a few feet away.

I see she's gotten off her chair, but she stops the instant Helga turns her attention to her. I see the girl's throat work as she swallows in fear of the woman.

"Did I tell you to get up?"

"He'll get less if she has marks. She's swollen," Mara tries.

Helga walks toward her. "Did I tell you to get up?"

"No, Ma'am." She lowers her gaze to the floor.

"You've just bought her six more lashes. Unless you'd like to take them in her place."

Mara looks up at her, then at me, tears in her wide eyes. Her lip trembles. This is what they've done to her these years? This child?

"Do you get off on this?" I call out to Helga. "Does it turn you on to look at helpless girls, Helga?" she turns her attention back to me, rage boiling inside her making her cheeks burn an angry red. "Are you going to fuck yourself when you're done? Come thinking of how my pussy looked when you strapped it?"

She walks back to me. If the first six were painful, I know the next will be hell. But it's worth it. I can't let her touch Mara. I would rather die than let her do that.

So, I take it. I take the lashes and I clench my jaw so as not to cry out, but I can't help my tears.

When it's over, I'm lifted up off the bed and carried into the bathroom. It's a good thing, I guess. My legs won't quite work as I process the still-throbbing pain. There, I'm submerged into a tub of too-hot water, doubling the sting.

"Bind her hands in front of her. I'm certainly not paid to clean that filth."

One of the guards does as she says, taking off the

cuffs and re-cuffing them with my arms in front. It feels better at least. Easier on my shoulders.

Helga stands over me and grins, hooking the strap back on her belt. She leans toward me.

"Give me any trouble and your next punishment will make this one look like a walk in the park."

I don't answer with words. It'd be stupid to. But I tell myself I'm going to kill her if I get the chance. Even if it's the last thing I do, because this is looking more and more hopeless the longer I'm here.

Cristiano is dead. No one is coming for me and there are enough soldiers out there to hunt me down or outright kill me. Even if I managed to get out of the house, I'm not valuable to them anymore. Maybe I'd be better off dead if I think about the alternative Felix has in store for me.

No. Dead is never better. Isn't that what Cristiano always says?

Said.

Not says.

Not anymore.

She straightens, gestures to one of the men to give her the shower gel and shampoo.

"Now get out," she snaps at the men.

The men look at each other like they're confused.

She looks up at them as she sets the things on the ledge along the tub. "I said get out. Are you as stupid as you are ugly or just hard of hearing?"

"We're to stay—"

"You can wait outside. I don't want you near Lizzie and you've certainly had your eyeful of this one." She turns her attention to me, looking like she's disgusted as the men clear out. "Come back in fifteen minutes to take her to the waxing room.

Waxing room?

She turns back to me. "Get to work."

I pick up the loofah.

CRISTIANO

"We have a lead on David," Antonio announces as I turn away from the woman in frustration. Her English is broken but from what she's telling me, she's one of the women they'd trafficked at some point. Terrified out of her mind, she keeps making the sign of the cross every time she glimpses either of the dead men, a stream of words in a language I don't understand pouring from her.

"They brought me to make the food," she repeats again. "But the girl doesn't eat." When I turn away, she continues to tell one of the soldiers. "I go now," she says, nodding as if giving herself permission to leave.

"Where?" I ask Antonio.

"Hotel in Amsterdam. I can get you there in forty minutes."

"Does he know we found him?"

Antonio shakes his head. "The man who just delivered his dinner called. Soldiers are on their way, but it'll be about twenty minutes before they're on site."

"Let's go," I say, then glance at the woman who has started sobbing again. One of the soldiers is holding on to her. She's not struggling against him, but she wants out. "Let her go," I tell him.

We file out of the decrepit house and back to our vehicle. With traffic, it takes us almost an hour to get to the hotel where, according to Antonio's contact, David checked into the Presidential suite for one night under an alias. That alias has a first-class seat booked on a plane heading to Dubai first thing in the morning.

"Does he have men with him?" I ask as we enter the property.

"No. Not that my contact has seen."

"Anything else on the location of that auction?" I ask for the hundredth time even though I know Antonio would tell me the instant he knew anything.

"Not yet."

The three of us ride up on the elevator accompanied by two soldiers.

"He'll know," Dante says.

I look at him, see the furrow between his brows. He's processing all this. Processing our uncle's betrayal.

He runs a hand through his hair and looks at me. I get that he's feeling responsible for allowing Scarlett to have been taken. He is, on some level. He should have protected her. But I also understand why he didn't.

"He'll know where she is. He doesn't leave loose ends," he adds.

"Aren't we loose ends?" I ask him.

His gaze darkens and he shakes his head. "It doesn't make sense, Cris. Makes no fucking sense."

I nod because he's right. It doesn't make sense that he'd massacre our family and leave us alive when he could easily have killed us. Me at least. I lay helpless in a coma. Dante too. Dante trusted him. We both did. It would have been easy for him. What was there for him to gain by keeping us alive apart from having me become his personal killing machine when someone crossed him?

"He's going to explain it to us now, Brother."

The elevator lets us off at the twenty-second floor. There are two doors in the hallway. Two suites. One is empty. Or was until I booked it. I won't take a chance that we're interrupted.

"How are we doing this?" Antonio asks when we step off the elevator.

I turn to him. "We're not. Dante and I are. And we're walking right up to the door and knocking."

"Are you sure that's a good idea?" Antonio asks, clearly, he doesn't think so.

"I'm sure."

Antonio and the soldiers flank us as we walk to the double doors of my uncle's suite. Once there I raise my hand and knock.

"It's about time," my uncle's voice carries before he even opens the door. "Does your chef know what rare—"

He's mid-sentence when the door opens. He looks pissed off, holding a plate with a steak on it, the piece of meat sliced in two sitting in its own bloody juices.

My mouth moves into a smile of its own accord. I don't feel it though. What I feel is a hardening in my chest. A deadening. Because when I look at this man, all I see are the bodies of my family lying on that bloodied marble floor.

"Uncle," I say as he looks first at me, then at Dante.

For a brief moment, I see that we've surprised him. That he truly did not expect us.

"Cristiano!" He smiles wide, sets the dish down on a side table. "I thought you were dead!"

"Hm." He almost moves in as if to hug me, but I push past him into the suite. Dante follows. Antonio and the soldiers stand sentry at the door as Dante closes it.

"Steak not rare enough?" Dante asks peering at it. "Looks good and bloody to me."

I take in the large room, the wall of windows, the

river that separates North Amsterdam from the center. All the lights, the lives being lived oblivious to what happens under their unsuspecting noses.

Scarlett is out there somewhere. Alone. Unprotected from men like my uncle.

I turn to face him. "Where's my wife?"

"Scarlett?" He glances at Dante but only momentarily as he addresses me with his answer. "I gave her back to Felix. Unharmed. I thought you were dead, Cristiano. I needed to protect Dante. She was a peace offering."

"It didn't look very peaceful on the video you left behind."

"That was Felix. Not me."

"You told me my brother was dead," Dante says.

"I thought he was," he says like he's confused by the question.

"No. The soldier who passed the news on, told you I was injured but stable," I tell him. "I don't have time for this. Where's my wife?"

"I don't know. I took her to the address Felix specified and from there, I don't know."

I remember Scarlett talking about how calm she remained in violent situations. How her heartbeat didn't even accelerate. She thought she might be a monster. I told her she wasn't. I stand by that.

Because I'm looking at the real monster. His mouth is moving but all I hear is the sound of bullshit. "I don't even know why you—"

I take hold of his arm, drag him to the desk in the corner and slam his hand flat onto it before taking the letter opener and stabbing it through the back of his hand with so much force, so much rage, that the wood splinters as the blade penetrates the desktop.

My uncle's scream is choked like it's caught in his throat. His eyes widen to stare at his impaled hand, at the blood seeping from it, at me.

"Where. Is. My. Wife?"

He turns from me to Dante who is watching from a few feet away. Dante picks a French fry off a dish beside my uncle's half empty glass of wine. He dips it in mayonnaise and eats it like it's the most normal, casual situation.

"That's nasty," he mutters, eating another one without the mayo. "I'd heard the Dutch eat their fries with mayonnaise, but I didn't believe it. Why would anyone do that?" He picks up the bottle of wine, pours some into an empty water glass and swallows it down like it's water.

"Cristiano," my uncle starts but stops. His eyes are shiny like he's on the verge of tears.

"You lied to me," Dante says, bringing the dirty steak knife over, anything casual gone from his face, his voice. "You fucking lied to me and I broke my promise to my brother. That part is on me. I'll pay for that. But the rest, that's all you. Now answer his fucking question or put your other hand on the desk," he says. "It's going to get messy." He shifts his gaze momentarily to my uncle's bleeding hand. "But you like messy, don't you?"

I wonder how Dante knows that detail but it's true. It's what my uncle always asked of me when I took out those names he listed for me. How many innocents have I killed for him?

"You too?" my uncle says to Dante. "You'll side with him as he accuses me when all I was doing was protecting you?"

"If you were protecting me, why are you here in Amsterdam registered at a hotel under a false name? Why would you run? Why would you hide unless you knew he was alive, and he'd come after you?" Dante pauses. "*We'd* come after you. It looks bad, Uncle, so help yourself out. Tell us where Felix took Scarlett. Then you can explain the rest of it."

"I need to sit down," David says.

Dante pulls the chair out, moves it around the desk and shoves it under him.

David sits, tucks his free hand into his pocket and takes out a handkerchief to wipe his forehead.

He looks up at Dante, smiles a little, the look on his face strange before he turns his attention to me, that expression different, colder.

"I could have let you die, I didn't. It would have been better for Dante if I'd let you die but I saved your life because he wanted me to. I did it for him."

"What do you mean it would have been better for me?" Dante asks.

I can't peel my eyes from him. This man who, if what Rinaldi says is true, masterminded my family's massacre.

"You don't know anything. Neither of you. You never knew your father, not really. How ruthless he could be. Only Michael saw that side of him. And you never knew your mother, either."

I fist a handful of his hair, tug his head backward and lean my face close to his. "Then educate us because you know what Rinaldi told me before I put his own knife in his throat? He told me about the message you wanted him to deliver. The last words my mother heard before he slit her throat."

Was it the same knife, I wonder? Did I kill him with the same blade he used to kill my mother?

Now comes the emotion. The elevated heart rate. I guess I'm not as much a monster as this man if I can still feel.

He snorts, face contorting a little in pain. "Rinaldi? That's where you're getting your facts from?" He raises his free hand when he says facts to make a single air quote. The instant he does, my brother grabs it, sets it beside the other and drives the steak knife through it.

No choked, shocked silence this time. My uncle screams.

"What did you do?" Dante demands with a roar.

"I did it for you, you ungrateful bastard! She would have gotten rid of you, but I told her no! I saved your fucking worthless life!" He draws a deep, shuddering breath in as tears begin to stream down his face. "You think she ever loved your father? Really loved him?" His eyes are on me now. "She loved *me* first. Me! Until my brother saw her and just like with everything else, he stole her too. And your mother..." he shakes his head, words foaming at his lips. "He turned her head. Stupid girl. Stupid, stupid girl." He shifts his gaze to Dante again. "I made sure you were off the island. I made sure you weren't anywhere near that charity event. I made sure you were protected from him. From the violence *he* brings."

The *he* my uncle is referring to is me. And the way he says it, the way he nods his head gesturing to me when he does, betrays his hate of me.

"You think that woman wanted to suck off an inexperienced fifteen-year-old boy? *I* arranged that. *For you.*"

Dante stumbles backward a step. His face contorts like he's just figured something out.

"Why?" he asks, so much emotion in those three letters.

"Why? Look in the mirror and tell me what you see," my uncle says to him.

Dante's hands fist at his sides.

I take hold of the hilt of the steak knife and pull it out, freeing one of David's hands. He gasps with the movement. I'm sure it's as painful coming out as it is going in. He starts to draw his arm back, but I grab it, turn it over and stretch it across the desk. I set the point of the knife at his wrist and push the sharp blade in. It cuts skin like butter and blood pours from his vein.

"You had him rape her. That's how you knew," I say.

"What?" Dante asks. He doesn't know this part. No one knew but me. I was the sole witness.

"You had Rinaldi rape our mother," I say again, out loud. It feels good to say it to him because he is more guilty than Rinaldi.

I push the knife deeper, feeling my own rage.

"Why?" I ask.

He drags his gaze from the knife up to me. He looks old. Already dead. "She accused me of it. I wanted to be sure she knew the difference," he spits. He shifts his gaze to Dante. "She couldn't love you because of it. She would have gotten rid of you. She needed to be punished. They all did. I did it for you. *For you.*"

Shock registers on Dante's face. His mouth opens, closes, opens again. "No." Dante shakes his head, backing away as he does. "No."

No.

I turn from my brother to my uncle. I stare in disbelief for a long, long moment. Because I'm registering too. "You fucking bastard. You god damned mother fucking bastard." Rage amplifies my voice. I start to slice the vein open. I want it to be painful. Slow. But I need something from him and all of this, all of what he is saying now, I need to wait to process it. It needs to wait.

"Where is my wife?"

"I loved her, don't you see?" he asks me, then turns to Dante. "Don't you see?"

"Where is my fucking wife?" I scream, stabbing the knife through his wrist and pinning it to the desk.

Dante is behind him in the next instant, gun cocked and at his temple. "Where is she, you bastard?" his voice is somehow controlled. "Where. Is. Scarlett?"

Our uncle, *my* uncle—he's something else to Dante, turns to Dante, gives him a grin. "You were never worth it."

My brother pulls the trigger.

SCARLETT

She leaves the door open so I can see a part of the bedroom and hear clearly. I scrub my hair as I listen to her talk to Mara, chastising her for not being in her seat. She was at the window.

"Let's get you changed. Mr. Petrov will be here soon."

"Do you know him?" Mara asks her as she undresses her before dressing her again in a pretty pink dress hanging in a garment bag from the closet door.

"No, of course not. But he's paid handsomely for you. Just look at this dress he sent."

"It's very pretty," Mara deadpans. I can see her face from here. She hasn't even looked at it.

"And look at this. There's even a teddy bear for you."

"I'm fifteen. I don't play with teddy bears," Mara says.

"You'll accept it and be grateful for it. Now sit."

"Do you know how old he is?"

"Why would his age matter? Silly girl. Now sit down so I can arrange your hair the way he wants it."

Mara turns to look at Helga, who has her back to me. Her eyes catch mine for just a brief moment. "I'm scared," she tells the woman.

Helga sighs. "Nonsense. He's been looking for someone like you for years. I'm sure he'll take good care of you. You'll be his little doll and he'll look after you just like Mr. Pérez does."

"That's what I'm scared of."

"Do I need to get the strap, Lizzie?"

"No, Ma'am."

"Good. Now sit down so I can do your hair."

Fucking bitch. She knows exactly what this Petrov is going to do to her. She knows exactly what he wants her for. And she's preparing her for him.

Sick.

"Five minutes," Helga calls over her shoulder, her tone entirely different when she talks to me.

"Almost done," I say as I look at her broad back, her thick hands braiding Mara's hair. There's a small mirror in front of Mara and I can see her face, see her looking down at the stuffed bear while Helga tugs and twists.

I climb out of the tub and grab a towel, wrapping it around myself as best I can with the cuffs binding my wrists. I pad into the bedroom.

Helga is finished with the first braid and is working on the second one.

Outside the door I hear footsteps, two men laughing, and a woman maybe. Mara hears it too. I see it in her worried expression.

Holding the towel to myself I look at the nightstand, at the lamp there. I wonder how much it weighs. It looks heavy, unwieldy, but I could manage. Even with the cuffs, I can manage it.

"Almost done," Helga says. "Sit still."

I reach behind the nightstand to unplug the lamp and pick it up to test its weight, as I pull off the shade.

I have nothing to lose but my life and isn't that gone anyway? Dead woman walking.

I turn to Helga just as she finishes the second braid. She backs up a step to look at her work and Mara's eyes meet mine in the mirror as I approach.

The floor creaks just as I'm a step away and Helga begins to turn.

"Oh no!" Mara cries out, dropping the bear, drawing Helga's attention just as I raise the lamp and bring it crashing down on the back of Helga's skull.

37

CRISTIANO

I look at my brother. He's still got the gun pointed at my uncle's head. Or where his head was. What's left of it is hanging backward and sideways. The knives pinning his hand and wrist to the desk are the only things keeping him in that chair that somehow hasn't toppled.

The door opens and Antonio steps inside. He stops, takes in the situation, expression unchanging like this is something you'd see every day.

Unruffled, he pulls out his phone and turns slightly away to make a call.

"Are you all right?" I ask Dante.

He looks at me, confusion and disbelief in his eyes. He takes a breath in, nods his head.

"Give me the gun," I say, holding out my hand.

"I'm fine," he says, holding it by his side. It's his first kill as far as I know.

Antonio disconnects the call. "Cleaner will be here in one hour."

"Thank you." I turn to my brother. "Give me the gun, Dante, and go wash your hands and face."

He tucks the gun into its shoulder holster, takes a deep breath in. "We need to find Scarlett," he says and walks to the kitchen, shoulders straightening as he does, as he washes his hands then splashes water on his face. He turns back to us as he wipes his face with a kitchen towel. He looks at the back of our uncle's head.

"I'm sorry—"

"It's not your fault. He deserved that."

He meets my gaze. "You didn't let me finish. I'm not sorry I killed him. I'm sorry I did it before he told us where Scarlett is."

I study him. I'm thinking about what David said. What he implied about Dante. What Dante must be processing.

But now isn't the time.

Antonio is already looking through David's pockets and a moment later he has the phone in his hand.

"I'll check the bedroom. See if he has anything that'll tell us."

I nod. Antonio and I watch him walk away and when he's gone, Antonio turns to me.

"Is he okay?"

"I doubt it. He probably shouldn't be alone," I

say, my eyes on the empty space at the end of the hall where my brother disappeared. My brother whom I wanted to protect from this. Protect from everything since I woke up from that coma. "We need to regroup. Get a location on that auction. The rest we'll deal with after."

Antonio is already working the phone. "Any idea what his password would be?"

"Call Charlie." I walk toward the room my brother entered. I find Dante rifling through papers and clothes he's dumped out of David's single suitcase. It's nothing more than an overnight bag. He rushed.

"He has another phone," Dante says without looking at me. "He's been fooling us all these years. Me longer than you."

"Hey."

"Ten years I spent with the man who killed my family."

"Dante."

He swipes papers off the bed with an angry sweep of his arm.

"Hey." I touch his shoulder, but he shrugs me off. "What?"

"He's a liar. We know that. What he said—"

"Mom was raped," he spits the words but at least he's finally looking at me. "You knew it and you never told me."

"You didn't need to know."

"Well, it seems I kinda did, considering the bit of news *Uncle* David just shared."

"I told you he's a liar."

"He's not lying about this," he says, shifting his gaze to the mess on the bed. He pulls his hand through his hair, tugging hard, taking a deep breath in. "We need to find Scarlett now. I let him take her. I need to get her back."

"It wasn't your fault."

"It was my fault. You know it as well as I do so let's move on."

Something in the jumble of papers on the floor catches my eye. I bend to pick it up. It's a black business card with three letters embossed in gold across the front.

I V I

"What is it?" Dante asks as I straighten.

I turn it over to look for more details but there's nothing. "I don't know."

He takes it from me. "I V I."

"Do you know it?"

He shakes his head but looks thoughtful. "Maybe." The phone in Dante's hand vibrates with a text message. It's from a contact with the initial X.

Petrov's entourage arrived. The address is at the fucking end of the world. Eindhoven. Willemstraat 13.

Antonio walks in then. "Charlie's working on the password. He's got—"

I take the phone out of my brother's hand and

turn to Antonio. "Willemstraat 13. Eindhoven. What's there? And who's Petrov?" I ask as the screen goes dark. When I hit the button to bring it back up, it's black, the phone password protected.

"Charlie?" Antonio asks, putting Charlie on speaker.

"Private residence on several acres of land surrounded by forest." I can hear him typing.

"Sounds like it's private enough to hold a human auction."

"That it is. No one actually lives at the estate apart from a caretaker and his wife. No neighbors for miles. It's perfect."

"I'm guessing we'll need more soldiers," I say, but Antonio's already on his phone.

"On it."

"Let's go."

38

SCARLETT

Helga stumbles backward, the sound she makes, the low keening, strange, almost inhuman. She catches herself on the vanity as Mara scrambles out of the way.

My towel has fallen. I stand over the woman naked and raise the lamp again. I bring it down harder on her forehead. Blood splatters across the mirror and she drops to her knees, eyes unfocused, mouth open but no sound coming.

Mara, who has backed away a few steps drops to her knees to stare at the woman.

"Again," she says.

I glance at her but she's staring at Helga. Helga turns her head to look at Mara.

"Again," Mara repeats. "Harder."

I bring the stand down one last time and this

time, she falls backward, her bulk shoving the vanity, dropping a perfume bottle onto the carpet.

Mara crawls toward her, peers at her face. She sits back on her heels and looks up at me. She smiles and begins to rock.

"He'll hurt you," she says to me.

I drop down to my knees too, cover myself with the towel then take her hands. "Mara?"

She blinks, looks up at me. I see how her eyes glisten with unspent tears. A decade's worth of tears. Her mouth opens and for a second, I think I see a flash of something, someone else in her eyes. But then it's gone, and she shakes her head.

"I'm Elizabeth," she says.

"No. Elizabeth is dead. You're Mara. I know your grandmother, Lenore."

She shakes her head again and shifts her gaze to the dead woman. "I'm Elizabeth," she says again while she undoes the strap that Helga had tied to her belt. "Elizabeth. Sometimes Lizzie. Never Mara."

She takes the strap, curls it up and tucks it into the pocket of her dress. A dress for a much younger girl. She then moves to Helga's pockets and from inside she takes a candy bar and what looks to be a small army knife. She flips the tiny blade open, tests the tip more deftly than I'd think she'd know how and tucks those away too.

"The windows are locked but you should go. You'll have to use the door," she says to me as she gets to her feet. "He can't punish me. I don't belong to him anymore."

"You don't belong to anyone," I say, rising too. "I know Elizabeth's family. Her brothers."

She stops, turns to me. "I told you. *I'm* Elizabeth. If you say I'm Mara, he'll be even angrier and then he'll punish you. You need to go now. Before he sees," she says as she takes a seat on the chair she'd been instructed to sit on before. I realize what I've just done, wondering if I've put her in even more danger than before.

More footsteps sound on the other side of the door. I look from it to her. She's humming a tune, a strange, creepy little lullaby.

"Sweetheart," I say, walking to her. I wipe the few drops of blood that got on her face off. "What did they do to you?"

The door opens then, and I spin around.

Two soldiers enter followed by Felix and another man. A big man. He's in a suit that barely contains him. He looks a little older than Cristiano. He has blond hair and blue eyes that are so pale they're almost eerie to look at.

They take in the woman lying on the floor. Felix's eyes land on the lamp, then me.

"What did you do?" he asks through clenched teeth.

The man beside him laughs outright. He pats Felix on the shoulder and Felix looks so small next to him. "You have trouble, Felix," he says with an accent that I'm pretty sure is Russian.

"No trouble I can't handle," Felix spits, eyes on me.

The man, what was his name? Petrov? Yes. Petrov's eyes land on Mara who is still sitting in her chair. He smiles at her. "Do you like my gift, little doll?" he asks her, his tone different when talking to her.

It makes my stomach turn.

"I'm too old for teddy bears," she tells him outright.

Felix mutters a curse and takes one step toward Mara, but Petrov catches him by the shoulder.

"What would you like then, little doll? What would make you happy?"

She just stares at him, her face expressionless.

"Tell me what gift you'd like," he says.

"A gift?" she asks him, standing.

He nods, appraising her. "Name it. It will be yours."

"I can have anything I want?"

I stand by and watch this, unsure what the hell is going on.

"Anything."

"Don't let him punish her." She points to Felix.

My gaze snaps to Mara as Petrov's lands on me. He walks toward her. I go to move between them, but someone grabs my arm to hold me back.

He's a fucking giant. He towers over her.

"That's what you want? You can have anything. That's what you ask for?"

She nods.

"And you'll be my good little doll if I give you what you want?"

She nods again.

"No, Ma—"

Mara's gaze snaps to me, quieting me, and I see not a little girl in her eyes but someone much older. A survivor. One so brutally damaged, so broken, I'm not sure she can be unbroken.

She looks back up at Petrov. "Will you give me that?" she asks, her tone suddenly sweet.

He smiles dotingly, nods once, turns to face Felix, his hand wrapping possessively around the back of Mara's neck.

I want to kill him. I want to lunge at him. Because men like him deserve to die.

"This is Grigori's wife?" Petrov asks although I'm pretty sure he knows.

Felix nods.

Petrov looks at me, appraises me, nods. "Felix won't touch a hair on her head, will you, Felix?"

Felix shifts his gaze to me, hate in his eyes, and I hear the wording, the exact and deliberate formation of Petrov's sentence.

"I will not touch a hair on her head," Felix

repeats, eyes narrowing, a wicked little grin twisting his lips.

"Then we shall take our leave," Petrov says. "Come," he tells Mara.

Mara turns to me. She gives me a strange, crooked smile and something inside me constricts because I know what will happen to her. I think she does too. And there won't be a thing I can do to stop it.

I watch him walk her out of the room. Felix keeps a smile pasted on his face as they disappear. He then turns to walk toward me.

"How could you do that? Let him take her? She's a little girl. Just a little girl."

"She's not your problem. In fact, you have much bigger problems to worry about, Cousin." He nods to the man who has hold of me. The soldier starts to walk me out of the room.

"You promised not to hurt me! Let me go!"

"I will keep my promise. Just like I kept my promise to let your husband know Marcus Rinaldi's location."

I stop. "You did that?"

He nods.

"You set him up?"

This time he smiles. "I always keep my promises, Cousin."

We step out into the hallway just as another door

opens and another woman, one I vaguely recognize from the boat is escorted out.

"Let me go!" I fight the guard now, knowing Felix sent Cristiano to his death. Knowing I'll join him soon.

"I won't touch a single hair on your head," Felix continues calmly as if I haven't spoken at all. He turns to walk in the opposite direction.

39

SCARLETT

Over the next twenty minutes two men keep me down while three women do their work. One waxes me to within an inch of my life. The only hair left on my person is that on my head and my eyebrows. I'm beyond feeling embarrassed at this point. I'm just fighting and I manage to kick one of the women in the nose. I'm pretty sure I break it, but I don't care.

Finding me too much trouble to apply makeup like they have to the other women, they brush out my hair and leave it loose down my back before attaching heavy cuffs to both my wrists and ankles then securing my arms at my sides by chains that attach to the ankle restraints. My ankles are connected too, by a short chain that makes every step a hazard.

There are more than a dozen women in here

with me. I recognize a few of the younger ones from the boat. We're all naked, my towel long gone. I'm the only one whose chains connect at the ankles, though. Theirs lock their arms to their sides but give them some mobility.

They're heavily made up, each more beautiful than the last. Each more terrified than the last. We're made to walk down a long, narrow corridor that's dimly lit toward the single door at the end.

It's loud in here. The sound of our chain gang reverberating off the walls.

An armed soldier leads the procession with several to accompany us. Although I hear some of the girls sniffling, no one cries outright, no one screams, no one tries to run.

No one but me. Not the running part, though. My goal is not escape. My goal is damage. Do as much damage as I can to the men and women who allow this. Make as much noise as I can. Do whatever I can to let these girls know someone will fight for them at least.

I doubt it'll give them hope, though. I think that's been beaten out of them.

But what happens after tonight?

What happens to them when I'm gone?

What happens to Mara who tried to save *me*? She has no idea what she's up against. The man who took her, the men I can now hear on the other side of that door, they're predators.

And watching their prey, terrorizing their prey, that's half the fun.

We come to a stop once we reach the door. I can hear the same music from when we first arrived, and the waiter was returning to the kitchen to replenish his tray of drinks. It's pretty and elegant and doesn't belong here. Not to these men. Not to this setting. Not to us in our chains.

"Where's Felix?" I ask the guard who still has my arm. He hasn't let it go for what feels like hours and I'm sure it's already black and blue.

He doesn't answer me.

Hell, he doesn't even look at me.

"Do you know who I am?" I ask him in Spanish, thinking maybe he doesn't speak English.

He glances down at me, eyes cold and hard, then shifts his gaze to the door again.

"I'm Scarlett De La Cruz. Manuel De La Cruz's daughter. I'm Cristiano Grigori's wife. His fucking wife. And when he finds out what you're doing to me, he'll kill you!"

My heart twists because he won't find out. And he won't kill anyone.

He's dead. Felix made sure of that when he gave him Marcus's location. Was it an ambush? Did he have a fighting chance?

All I get for my effort is a tightening of his grip.

I wince but soon my attention is drawn to the door that opens. Soft light pours into the corridor and a severe looking woman wearing a depressing gray suit looks from her clipboard to us. All the way down the line, she glances at each of the girls, then me. She doesn't linger on any of us though. Instead, she points to the first girl, checks something off her clipboard and gestures for the girl to be brought after her.

The girl resists but only momentarily because she isn't given the time to fight. She's taken through that door and it's closed. We all stare after her, all of us quiet.

I strain to hear the sounds on the other side of that door but it's the same. Nothing different. Soft music. Men's quiet voices.

But after a moment, it changes.

The music is gone, a gong struck, the hum of conversation ended.

A man's voice then announces the auction is about to begin.

I swallow hard at the thought. It's not easier or less terrifying even knowing that it doesn't matter what happens to me anymore. I'm still afraid. And as much as I want to focus on the other girls, there's a part of me that's just too scared.

The auction begins. I know from the sound of the man running it. It's so strange, it could be an auction for a piece of art or for a container on those TV shows or for a freaking cow. Nothing differentiates it from those things. The fact that there's a human being, a girl out there being held against her will, being sold, it doesn't matter to these men.

I know that, though, don't I? Haven't I lived with monsters all my life?

We're not human to them. And if we were, we wouldn't hold any more value than a cow. Maybe less.

The gavel comes down, someone hoots, and there's the sound of clapping. So civilized.

The door opens and the woman with the clipboard gestures for the soldier to hurry the next girl out. We all shuffle forward.

The girl in front of me pulls back but it doesn't matter. These men holding us, they're so much stronger than us and there's too many of them.

No gong this time but I hear a joint sound of male appreciation.

One of the girls starts to cry and another joins in. The hammer comes down marking the end of the auction and again the door opens, the next girl taken out.

This time, though, the woman returns before the end of the auction followed by another woman, the same one who greeted us in the kitchen. Their drab suits match, I realize, and they both look less than pleased.

"Which one started the crying fest here?" she asks, eyes on the girls.

I Thee Take

The guard who is responsible for the guilty one, pushes his charge forward.

The woman steps toward her, cocks her head to look at her then touches her face, wiping away a tear. "Look what you've done to your face. Your makeup will have to be fixed. The others too."

The girl swallows standing suddenly, very straight. I realize why when I see how the woman with the clipboard is holding her chin, nails digging into skin.

"But there's always one example to be made," the woman says and gestures to the other woman to step forward. "I'm going to give you a choice. Each of you sobbing will have the same choice to make if you're still crying like babies when I'm finished with this one."

The one from the kitchen steps forward and raises her hand to show what she's holding. It's a large wooden paddle that I imagine can do real damage.

"We'll need to make sure our customers understand there's a reason you're crying. Six strokes of the paddle will do it. Or."

She gestures to the other woman again who raises the other hand. This one is gloved and holding a long, bulbous item. It takes me a minute to register.

"We can let them know we're stretching a tighter than usual anal passage for their pleasure."

The girl tenses her buttocks and I realize no one is making a sound now. Not a single one of them. Not even me.

"You have until I finish my sentence to choose your punishment or you'll get both."

"Please—"

"Both it is then."

"Paddle!"

The woman with the clipboard smiles at her, almost kindly. I swear she's the devil. She releases her and nods to the kitchen woman.

"Turn around and touch your toes. If you rise before you're given permission, she'll begin all over again."

The way we're all bound, I realize it still allows them access to us in any position they need us.

The girl nods, starting to cry again.

"Don't ugly cry. That won't sell."

The girl turns, bends and touches her toes. I get the feeling this isn't the first time they've done this but there's still a collective gasp at the sound of the first paddle stroke. The girl, to her credit, doesn't make a sound though. She jumps with each stroke, the soldier having to hold onto her before she falls over.

When it's over, she is allowed to straighten, her face red as she faces us, eyes watery, knees wobbly.

"Anyone else?" the woman asks.

They all shake their heads.

"Didn't think so." She turns to the soldier. "Get her cleaned up."

He nods and the punished girl is whisked away. I don't miss the erection in the man's pants as he passes me.

Perv.

The gavel comes down then and everyone's attention returns to the door. It all goes much more quickly than I expect. One after another is taken through that door. The girl who received the punishment is the last to go before me, her makeup righted but not completely. Her bottom bright red for the marks.

When it's her turn, she disappears. I hear a howl from the men. I guess she'll bring in more with, than without, the marks. Felix will be pleased.

The woman with the clipboard returns before the gavel comes down and looks me over. She's unimpressed. But so am I.

"They're just girls," I say to her. I know it won't make a difference.

She meets my eyes. "But you're a woman. A woman with many enemies." She lifts my hair off my shoulders and sets it behind my back then looks me over. "Go," she tells the soldier holding me.

"Ma'am—"

"I said go. I'll bring her in. There are girls in the barn."

He licks his lips and from the look in his eyes I get the feeling he's anxious to get to the barn.

"If you're sure."

"I'm sure."

A moment later he disappears. The woman and I stand alone in the corridor.

"What do you want?" I ask her, knowing how helpless I am even against this woman who stands several inches shorter than me.

She tucks her hand into her pocket and brings it out, opening it to show me a pill in the palm of her hand.

"I'm no friend of Felix Pérez," she says.

"That doesn't make you my friend," I say, eyes on that pill. I know how these people use their words. Know they're all monsters.

"No, it doesn't," she says distastefully. "Your fate is sealed. You won't be walking out of here after this night. This will make it easier for you."

The capsule in her palm looks harmless but I'm sure it's not. "What is it?"

"Cyanide."

I shift my gaze back to hers. "You want me to kill myself?"

"It'll be the best death for you."

"And you're doing this to spare me?"

She snorts. "Of course not. There are men out there who have paid Felix well to attend this evening's event once they learned of your presence.

They'll be displeased because, well, like I said earlier, you have enemies."

"And you want my enemies to become Felix's enemies."

"Oh no, they're already that. I just want them to act on it."

"Why don't you swallow that pill. I'll take my chances with the snakes out there."

She gives me a one-sided grin. "Last chance."

"Alternatively, you could shove it up your ass," I say, somehow sounding much braver than I feel.

She closes her palm just as the gong goes off. "Looks like it's your turn."

40

CRISTIANO

"Any chance we can get eyes on the estate? Gauge what we're walking into," I ask Charlie as we drive toward the location in Eindhoven. I watch the dark sky, the raindrops only a nuisance on the windshield now. Clouds are rolling angrily in the distance, illuminated by still-silent flashes of light.

Antonio is coordinating more manpower and Dante is sitting beside me staring out the window, hands fisted.

"We can't get closer than the public road leading up to the house. They've got their own drones," Charlie says.

"Of course, they do."

I have him on speaker phone but I'm not sure Dante's listening.

"From what I've learned about past auctions,

they issue, at most, two dozen invitations. In most cases, the buyer himself doesn't attend. They send someone in their place. None of these men want to be in the same room together if they can help it. None of them want to be seen."

"Makes sense. How do they know what they're bidding on?"

"A brochure would have circulated prior to the event."

"A fucking brochure?"

"These are animals we're dealing with, Cristiano."

"Christ."

"It's a pretty sophisticated operation. These sort of auctions are extraordinary from what I'm learning. They'll save the special girls. Your uncle kept pretty good records from what I've found, and I get the feeling this is scratching the surface."

"Do you know what he did with the information?"

"Nothing yet. But you should see what he's got. Who he's got. It would surprise you. Although he wasn't on the cartel's payroll, he had plenty of ammunition to get what he wanted from a number of people in various countries at various levels of power."

"Dirty bastard."

"We walk in," Dante says.

Charlie stops talking.

I turn to my brother.

He looks determined. "You and me. We walk in like we're invited. Like we belong there. Once we have Scarlett, we'll need a distraction so we can get out."

I study him, head tilting as I think about this.

"They won't be expecting someone to walk through the front door. You and me walk in, Brother. We get Scarlett. Someone pulls a fucking fire alarm. I don't know. But we get out. We deal with the mess after. Once she's out of harm's way."

"That's risky," Charlie says. "But Dante may be right. It may be your best bet to get on property and get to Scarlett in time. There's a forest and a fucking stone wall once you cross the property. Getting in any other way will be difficult and we'd have to wait for soldiers to arrive on site."

"What do you want me to do, bid on my own wife?"

"We do what we need to do to get her out," Dante says. "Period."

"If our men aren't there by the time you get her, I'll call in a disturbance. Get the local police out there. They won't want the attention. The attendees will scatter like cockroaches," Charlie says.

I consider this. It could work. And it may be our only option.

"She may not have much time, Cristiano," Charlie adds as if he's just read my mind.

The driver takes the exit off the highway and a few moments later we're on a dark, single lane road, two cars close behind with soldiers. More coming from other directions but it'll take time and we're out of it.

"Pull over. We'll switch cars. Antonio and I will go in. Dante, you ride in the next car."

"No," Dante says.

"What do you mean no?"

"I mean I go in with you. It's my plan. I'm not sitting it out. And I want this."

"You're not trained well enough—"

"You really think I'm not trained? That for the last ten years since finding my family massacred, I haven't been preparing for a moment like this one? Like the one we just had? What kind of fool do you think me, Brother?"

I study him, my younger brother, my, what I presumed carefree brother, living the life he should live with girls and liquor and fun. Not the half-life of a damaged boy turned damaged man.

"Pull over," I tell the driver.

He does and we all step out. The rain's picked up and I'm getting wet but I'm still considering my brother. He needs this. I know it.

I nod. "I'm driving," I say. "Antonio, Charlie, I'll give the signal. You two work out the distraction."

41

CRISTIANO

Rain now drums against the roof of the car. The windshield wipers work frantically to clear the glass.

The street leading to the house is quiet. We're late to the party.

Dante is sitting beside me loading extra rounds of ammunition into his pockets. I keep looking at him to see if I can read distress, any sign of upset after what just happened. He's got the radio turned up to some heavy metal shit music and is focused on his Glock.

Narrow canals parallel the road on either side with trees lined up at the perfect distance from one another almost as if someone used a ruler when planting them.

As the road curves to the right, I see lampposts

along the side of the road. In the distance, the tall gates of the estate, the gargoyles perched atop the pillars on either side lit up like two devils.

I turn to Dante who is looking ahead at the entrance, too.

"Whatever happens, none of this is your fault. You know that, don't you?"

He turns to me. "You don't need to baby me, Brother."

"I'm not babying you. I know you're not a fucking baby. But you're still my kid brother. You'll always be my kid brother."

He studies me. "Nothing is going to happen," he says, turning back to the gates as we near them, turning the volume up on the radio when we see the first armed guards come into view. I slow the car, pushing the button to roll down my window part of the way, irritated by the rain pelting my face. Dante tucks his weapon out of sight and sings along to some of the lyrics. The guard leans his head down to look inside the vehicle as he pushes his automatic rifle behind his back.

"Gentlemen," he says. He has to scream it over the rain. Lightning electrifies the sky just beyond the hulking house.

Another man shines a flashlight inside checking out the backseat.

"This is a private residence. You'll need to turn

around." He's soaked, umbrella barely hanging on in the wind.

I turn the music down. "I expect Pérez to have booked a private residence considering."

He studies me as his colleague knocks on the trunk of the car.

"Why are you so late?"

"We got lost. This place is the fucking end of the fucking world and road signs don't exactly help when you don't speak the language."

"Name."

My brother turns the music back up and leans across to look at the man. "You don't recognize my brother? He's fucking famous."

The man looks from him to me. He gives up on the umbrella with the next gust of wind and tosses it aside, letting the rain cascade down his face. "Name."

Committed.

"Grigori," Dante says, sitting back in his chair as I survey what's beyond the gates. More armed soldiers, smoking, a few feet away. Lights from the house, about a mile farther down, and more than a dozen vehicles dotting the place. At least of those I can see.

"I gotta take a piss," Dante says to the man.

"Just a minute. Let the man do his job," I tell him.

"They could pay a fucking monkey to do this job

faster," he mutters half in English half in Italian. The monkey part loud and clear.

"What did you say?" the soldier asks.

The man at the back knocks his fist twice on the trunk.

"Pop the trunk," the one from the back yells.

I do. "Is there a problem?" There's nothing in there but a spare tire.

"Your name doesn't appear to be on my list," he says, eyes narrowing on us. His accent sounds local.

"Clean," the man at the back says, closing the trunk.

"Then your list is wrong." I turn to Dante. He's waiting for my signal. I need to get inside. If I have to kill these fuckers to do it, I will but I don't want to sound the alarm.

"I don't think..." the man starts then stops. "Shit!"

I follow his gaze to where another vehicle drives erratically toward us from inside the gates. It's a large SUV and I can only make out the shadows of the two in the front seat. The driver honks his horn angrily.

"Petrov," the one with the clipboard says.

"Mother fucker," the other one curses.

The driver lays on his horn opening his window and flipping us or the guards or the whole lot of us off as he barrels toward us and even over the music, I can hear him laughing.

"Fucking asshole," clipboard guy says as he jumps backward.

I hit the gas and pull through the gates, only managing to miss the SUV by a hair. In the rearview mirror I see it swerve as if to run over the soldiers.

"Who the fuck is fucking Petrov?" Dante asks.

"He's the asshole that got us in," I say once we're far enough away from the gates that I can't see the soldiers stationed there anymore.

"Two guards at the front door," Dante says.

I park the car where I have a clear exit, avoiding the collected SUVs and sedans with drivers sitting inside, smoking their cigarettes, smoke wafting out of the cracked open windows.

Lightning crashes over head as the lights blink once, twice. The soldiers at the door look at each other with uncertainty.

"Front door," Dante says, opening his door.

"Let's go get my wife."

We climb out of the car, adjust our jackets and walk at a normal pace through the rain. One of the soldiers tosses the butt of his cigarette, gives us a nod as the other opens the heavy door.

I make a note of the soldiers stationed inside as we enter a hallway where a woman stands ready to take our coats. Except, we're not wearing any. My brother gives her a nod and a wink. Women always liked Dante. He can be charming. When he wants.

I hear the sound of a harp. Pretty music. Soft

music. Music that doesn't belong here. It's coming from beyond the heavy curtains separating the vestibule from the room beyond.

The gong strikes as two women pull the curtains aside.

Dante and I stand side-by-side taking it in, the opulence, the excess. The money. So much money you can almost smell it.

Candles are being lit around the room. Backup I guess, as thunder claps and the lights dim then return.

We step in and the curtains are dropped behind us.

Men in suits stand talking, smoking cigars, drinking what I'm sure is the finest whiskey. About fifteen of them. Half that number are weaving through with trays of drinks and food. Six soldiers stand along the perimeter of the room.

The lights go down. This isn't because of the storm outside.

I notice the absence of women in here. Even the servers are men. When the gavel hits the podium, I shift my attention to the older man standing on the left of a small stage where the curtain is still down.

"Gentlemen," the man begins elegantly.

I take the opportunity to look around, searching for Pérez or anyone else I might recognize. I don't. But like Charlie said, these men are likely decoys sent in to make the purchase and keep the identity of the buyer secret.

"The final piece of tonight's auction. This is a special offering from our friend, Mr. Felix Pérez with slightly different rules."

Again, I look for him. For *our friend*. But he's nowhere to be found.

"She's a beauty, as you'll soon see..." he begins as the curtains lift and I see my brother watching the stage in my periphery. Every nerve ending in my body comes alive. As my blood begins to pump red hot through my veins, the drumming against my ears muffles Dante's muttered curse.

"She's a gift for you. Each of you. Here for your pleasure to close a successful evening," the man continues. The rising curtain reveals feet shackled together, the chain between them allowing only minimal movement, effectively hobbling her. Chain links climb along slender legs each binding a shackled wrist to those around her ankles.

"There's only one rule: take your fill."

There's a woot from the men as more of the woman is exposed.

"Highest bidder will have first use of her, then the second highest and so forth and so on until you've all had a turn. We'll begin the bidding in a moment once you've had a good look."

Her sex comes into view, the slit visible to the pleasure of the gathered men. Her flat belly is next, then her breasts, small and taut. Her face held high, hair behind her shoulders, cheekbone bruised where Felix had slapped her. The bright light is blinding her, making it impossible for her to see them. This sea of men.

Making it impossible for her to see me.

To see that I've come for her.

42

SCARLETT

"*You won't be walking out of here tonight.*"

Did she mean that literally? Because if this is Felix's plan for me, then I'll be fucked by every man out there in turn.

I hear the woot of the onlookers once the curtain is fully raised. I can't see much of them and I think that's on purpose. The spotlight follows me even when I turn my head.

A man calls out a ridiculous number and makes a lewd comment. Several laugh out loud as the auctioneer chuckles into his microphone, tapping his gavel twice to get everyone's attention.

"You haven't even seen it all yet," he notes in a sing-song voice.

Two sets of hands take hold of my arms and force me to turn. When they do, I catch a glimpse of the blinking red light coming from the top corner of the room.

Felix is recording this. Is it for me? Well, I should say is it for him? To show those who won't pledge loyalty to him what happens if you are his enemy? Or is it to hold onto after these men leave. Material to blackmail them when it suits him.

Not that it matters one way or the other for me. My ending doesn't change, camera or no camera.

The soldiers pull me forward making me bend all the way over. I fight but it's no use. I can see them now, the men in the room. The spotlight is on another part of my anatomy and now I can see their faces. There's more than a dozen of them.

The auctioneer describes my attributes as I'm held down. One of the soldiers twists his hand in my hair when I try to move, forcing my gaze into the room. I close my eyes, feel hot tears burn my face.

This is my end? Attacked by these men then murdered? Diego and Angel were lucky then.

I think about Cristiano. Dead already. I think about Noah out there. God, please let him be safe. Please don't let him be waiting for me. Searching for me.

I think about Mara with that man.

The things she has seen. The things she has yet to see.

I think about those other girls already sold tonight. And the barn the woman mentioned.

I steel myself, open my eyes just as I'm straightened, lifted, turned so quickly I stumble, dizzy with the rush of blood.

For a brief instant, my mind plays a trick on me. Because what I'm seeing can't be real. It can't be him. But there, for the briefest instant before the spotlight shines in my eyes, I see Cristiano.

I'd recognize his eyes in a crowd of a hundred. A thousand.

Cristiano.

I blink, try to see him again, but I'm blinded once more. All I can do is stand there and listen to the monsters call out numbers. Hear them buy parts of my body, my soul. Hear the gavel slam down as those sales are recorded.

And just as I'm lifted off the pedestal and carried off the stage, as if on cue, lightning crashes overhead and the lights go out.

43

CRISTIANO

The room goes sideways, my brain rattling against my skull.

Dante's hand closes swiftly over my shoulder. "Steady."

I fist my hands, clenching and unclenching, my blood boiling. I reach blindly for my gun.

"Hey." Dante steps in front of me, voice firm as he takes my arms and shakes me hard.

I blink. Focus my eyes.

The lights have gone out. The room is lit only by candles now. More are being lit around us.

My vision adjusts after a moment. When it does, I see the table in the far corner that had been unoccupied before, busy now. A man sits behind it punching numbers into a machine while another man dictates to him. One of the attendees.

"Good," Dante says. "Focus. You take your pistol out here and she's as good as dead."

I nod, my eyes on the back of the man paying for his turn at Scarlett.

"First. Lucky bastard," the accountant says, standing to shake the man's hand once the transaction is complete. "I hope there will be something left when I take a turn."

The man laughs, pats the accountant on the shoulder with a big, meaty hand. He must weigh four-hundred pounds.

"Carlos," the accountant calls. "If you'll show our guest the way."

Carlos steps forward, nods. He's a big guy and armed. He walks ahead of the fat man and they slip through a door at the far corner. Another solider promptly steps in front of the door to block anyone else from passing through.

I take another step toward it. Meet the soldier's eyes.

"Cris," Dante says, voice low but firm. "Focus."

I nod, turn to look around the room again. A door opens at the far end and one of the men reenters as he zips his pants.

"Let's go," I say as we move toward that unguarded door. We walk through and step into a corridor lit only by candles and the occasional flash of lightning from the window. Several doors line the corridor and I know the one I'm looking for is the one where a soldier stands guard.

"Bathroom," my brother says to him.

The man points to the opposite end of the hall and we walk in that direction. The door he's blocking is glass, so I can see the fat man when we pass. He's climbing some stairs at the far end.

"Gentlemen," the soldier says. "Move on."

I didn't realize I'd stopped. I shift my gaze to meet his. He's my height. My build.

"My brother drank a little too much," Dante says, coming to put an arm around me.

I wonder if I appear drunk. I'm not fully myself, that's for sure. My heartbeat is strong, loud in my ears, blood rushing. I have tunnel vision. I see one thing. Getting to that man. Getting to Scarlett.

The soldier nods, expression unchanging. He holds my gaze and folds his arms across himself.

I reach into my back pocket, using something out of Marcus Rinaldi's playbook, push the button on the switchblade and, without a moment's hesitation, push the blade into his gut.

He doesn't have time to blink before it happens. Before the knife is forced so deep in his stomach, I feel the soft, mushy insides against my hand.

I thrust deeper, getting close enough to hold him upright, one hand around his arm, my body pressing his to the door.

His eyes have gone wide, his hand frozen on its way to reaching for his weapon.

I twist once more, feel his full weight on me as his knees buckle. A choked sound comes from his throat before a trail of blood seeps from the corner of his mouth.

"Fuck," Dante says from behind me.

I pull the blade out, wipe it on the man's shirt as Dante catches his other arm.

"What about getting in, getting Scarlett and getting out?" he asks as we drag the man's heavy body to the bathroom.

"Fuck that."

"Oh yeah? And why is that? Because you want an army coming after us?"

"Because I'm going to kill every mother fucker in this place before I walk out tonight."

We drop him in the bathroom. Dante looks at me. He grins. "*We're* going to kill every mother fucker in this place. *We*, Brother."

44

SCARLETT

The chains that bind my wrists to my ankles are removed and my arms are stretched overhead, bound to a metal rung on the headboard. I'm flipped onto my stomach, the cuffs clanging as I'm tugged downward. The link that hobbled me is also removed. My legs are pulled apart, stretched to either corner of the bed and linked to the rungs there.

The two men responsible for preparing me, stand back and look down at me. One tugs the pillow out from under my head and shoves it beneath my belly. He nods, meets my eyes and cups his erection.

"I'll take your ass when it's my turn," he says in Spanish. "Save me a piece."

I spit at him.

He slaps my ass.

"Hey," the other soldier interrupts and points to the corner where I see one of those flashing red lights again. The camera is hidden but the soldiers know about it. They must be Felix's men. "After."

The man glances at the blinking light, nods then returns his attention to me. "If there's anything left."

They walk out but don't close the door. Instead, they stand in the hall looking at me as one lights a cigarette. I tug at my restraints but it's no use. I already know that.

Cigarette smoke wafts in from the hallway. I twist my neck to look toward the door, as the sound of another man, one with a hoarse voice and a heavy Russian accent floats into the room. It makes me think of Petrov. Of Mara.

But honestly, it's hard not to think about myself now. Maybe I should have accepted the pill from the bitch downstairs. Killed myself before they could have their fun.

I close my eyes and steel myself, or try to, as the voices grow closer. I know the man is standing just outside the door. I don't open my eyes. I don't want to. I can imagine the view.

They speak for a few minutes before I hear the door close and the man sighs deeply.

"A pretty gift," he says as the bed dips beneath his weight. He puts a hand on my hip.

"Don't touch me!" I hiss, tugging away the inch I'm able to.

"Oh, I will do more than touch you," he says, standing again, taking off his jacket. He tosses it over the back of a chair. He doesn't bother taking off his shirt. He just opens his belt, then the crotch of his pants. He fists himself.

I look at it, at his little dick barely visible under his grotesque belly, how it practically disappears in the palm of his hand. I grin, blink, and shift my gaze back up to his.

"Is that all?" I ask. I know it's stupid, but I can't help it. "I'm not sure I'll even feel that."

His hand stops moving. He releases his dick to grab a fistful of my hair and tug my head back painfully. "I'll pay extra to cut out your tongue once your mouth is used up."

"Be careful. Your dick is going flaccid."

He pushes my face into the pillow, smothering me. I fight as oxygen is cut off. I feel him climb onto the bed, feel the rough fabric of his pants brush the insides of my legs.

Just when I think I'll pass out, he releases my head and I gasp for breath. His hands are on my ass spreading me open.

"No!"

"Pretty little pussy you have here. Prettier than your mouth."

"Please!" I beg. I don't mean to. I don't want to. I know it will mean nothing to them. No, not nothing. It'll probably turn these men on. "Get the fuck off me, you asshole!" I shout instead, struggling against my bonds, trying to get away from him even though it's impossible.

I fight hard. I scream. I can't just take it. I won't.

When did I start to sob, though?

He tugs at my bonds, does something to stretch my legs so tight I can barely move an inch. I try again, though. Try to kick, to move. Anything.

"Better," he says.

A finger brushes my opening and I freeze.

"Please," my voice trembles.

He leans over me. "Not so tough now, are you?" he asks, breath hot and dank against my cheek.

I close my eyes and feel myself wilt. Because it's done. Finished. I drop my head.

"I didn't think so."

The door opens. Is it the next man early to take his turn?

But then I hear a grunt and feel the monster at my back. I can't think about anything else but the violation. I feel him against me, the bulk of him pressing heavy on my back, crushing me. I feel him, warm, wet, slimy, and slippery. All I can do is sob. All my strength, my fight has leaked out of me and all that's left are my sobs.

I hear a thud then. I look over to see what made that sound. It's the man. He's on the floor. It takes me a moment to register that he's gone from my back. To register that I can breathe again.

But other hands touch me then. The blanket tugged out from under me, tossed over me.

I scream as this next man takes his place.

I scream at the new assault to come.

"Fury." The word is spoken so quietly I'm not sure if it's real or just my mind playing tricks.

A hand cups the back of my head. I still. I can't move. Can't turn my head. Can't open my eyes.

Fury.

No, not Fury. Just a pathetic little kitten.

"Scarlett."

I stop breathing, more tears pouring.

It's Cristiano's voice.

But he's dead. Am I dead?

No. There's too much pain for that. The pain inside my heart the worst of it. Dead doesn't hurt, does it? It's an ending to pain, isn't it?

"Scarlett," he says louder.

I open my eyes but keep my gaze on the bed. I smell laundry detergent and that distinct metallic scent of blood. But there's something else. Something familiar.

"I need you to be my Fury now," he says, and I turn my head to look at him from the corner of my eye. Then tears come again. So many tears.

"You're dead," I manage, the words sticking in my throat.

He smiles, leans down to brush the hair from my face, pressing his lips to the top of my head.

"I'm not so easy to kill."

The lights blink on then and I realize the only light in the room was from the candles set along the perimeter.

"We need to move," someone says.

I turn to see Dante who makes a point of averting his gaze when the blanket slips away.

Cristiano gets up, pulls his shirt over his head and covers me with it.

"Keys?" he asks his brother.

Dante is going through the pockets of a jacket he's got in his hand. "Try these." He tosses them to Cristiano.

The third one on the ring works. Cristiano unlocks my ankles first, then my wrists. I sit up, looking at him. He adjusts the shirt he just tossed over me, pulling it over my head.

"I thought you were dead," I say as I wrap my arms around him, clinging to him. "I thought—" my voice catches. He holds me tight, hugging me into his chest, one strong arm around me the other around the back of my head. He lets me cry just for a minute. Just for the briefest moment.

"I need you to be my Fury now, Scarlett," he whispers.

I know what he means. I nod, try to pull myself together.

"Did he—" he stops, unable to say the rest of the words.

I shake my head. "I'm okay," I say. "He didn't..." I trail off looking at the dead man, realizing what that warm wetness was. Blood. His blood.

He stands and helps me up.

"Don't look at him. He doesn't deserve your gaze."

Dante reads something on his phone, and I see the Glock he's holding at his side.

"Our men are on the grounds, not in the house yet though."

I hear gunfire outside the house then and a moment later, a small explosion.

Cristiano goes to the window, one arm wrapped around me, as he looks out over the front yard. I see the men out there, the gunfight. I notice the fire at the far end of the house.

"We need to move," he tells Dante, then turns his attention to me. "Is Felix on site?"

"I don't know," I say.

He nods. "If he is, I'll find him. But I need to get you out first." He holds my hand, and we walk around the bed to where the dead man is lying face down in his own blood. He bends to tug his knife out of the man's side.

I notice the new injury on his side then. The bandage over the new set of stitches long gone. I touch it.

"You're hurt."

He takes my wrist, shifting his grip to my hand.

"It's nothing. Let's go. Once I get you out, I'll come back for Felix."

"Wait, Cristiano." I grab his arm when Dante opens the door.

Another explosion rocks the house and I let out a little scream.

"We have to go, Scarlett," Cristiano says with some urgency.

"Mara," I say.

Dante whirls to face me. A crease forms between Cristiano's eyebrows.

I look at them both. "She's alive. She's here. Or she was here."

"Alive?" Dante asks, taking a step toward me.

I nod. "A man called Petrov has her. He...bought her."

"Petrov?" Dante looks sick suddenly.

I nod.

"If Petrov has her, she's gone," Cristiano says. He turns to say something to Dante, but gunfire breaks out in the corridor and we duck to take cover.

Everything happens so fast then. So many men. So many shots fired. Heavy boots beat down the lush carpet as they rush through the halls. Cristiano drags me with him, refusing to let go of my hand as war breaks out inside the house.

I don't know who's who. I can't tell who's on our side, who's on theirs. And I feel like dead weight as Cristiano covers me again, shielding me from harm, putting his body in the way of any bullet that might come for me.

There's another explosion, this one closer, knocking out a door at the far end of the hall.

"Stairs," Cristiano calls out over the noise, pointing.

I recognize them. They're the stairs I climbed when we first got here.

"They'll take us to the kitchen!" I scream to Cristiano and Dante as soldiers bear down on us.

We get to an open door and Cristiano shoves me into the room, freeing himself to reload his weapon before stepping out into the hallway again.

"No!" I call out when I hear the bullets.

But a moment later, I see Dante. He's caught up to us. I hadn't realized we'd lost him. He switches out the Glock's magazine, turns and takes another shot. More boots charge up the stairs at the opposite end of the hall, running over the fallen bodies of soldiers.

We get to the stairs that lead to the kitchen and sprint down, Cristiano catching me when I fall.

"Get her out!" Cristiano yells to Dante, releasing me as soon as we're in the kitchen. From here I see the fire in one of the outbuildings.

Dante turns, sees something, and immediately throws himself in front of Cristiano. His body jerks violently and he stumbles back to the wall, stunned momentarily.

"No!" I cry out because a circle of blood is already seeping into his shirt at the center of his chest. "No."

Cristiano goes white when he sees his brother stumble, slide down a little. When he sees the smear of blood on the wall, that shock morphs into something else. Something powerful and violent and vengeful.

He is Fury now.

He turns to face the oncoming soldiers and I scream. I cover my ears and scream and scream. He kills every one of those men before one final, massive explosion rocks the house. The floor beneath us seems to sway, men falling, the click of an empty pistol loud in the moment before this tsunami touches down.

Cristiano turns to me, then to his brother.

Dante stumbles. Cristiano wraps one arm around him, the other around me, and we almost make it to the door before the house explodes around us.

45

CRISTIANO

Dying is a strange thing. To be half a part of this world half a part of another.

There's pain first. A burning, searing pain.

I look at my brother. He's still here. Feeling it. I see it in his eyes.

Then comes the buzz of noise as sound fades in and out. As you fight to understand. Fight to stay alive. To stay here.

Some people say they saw a light at the end of the tunnel. I didn't. I only remember the dark. If I believed in a god, I'd say it was his way of letting me know he doesn't want to have anything to do with me.

I touch my brother's face.

He turns his head a little to look at me.

I hope he sees the light. I hope...fuck...I hope there's light for him.

"Get them out!" Someone yells.

I look up, see Antonio. See soldiers. Ours. See the piles of dead bodies beyond. Beside me I see Scarlett. She's sitting up, hand to her head. Dazed, bruised and bloodied but alive and alert.

When she looks at me, her mouth opens, and I know she's screaming my name but it's all just white noise now.

When I look at Dante again his eyes have closed.

He's dying. Maybe I'm dying too.

Scarlett's hands turn my face, making me look up at her. I reach up to touch her cheek. Smear away blood. So much blood.

She's the last thing I see before I close my eyes. And I try to tell her I'm sorry.

Because I told her I'm not so easy to kill. But maybe I've used up my lives.

46

SCARLETT

I carry two cups of coffee into Dante's room. Cristiano is sitting across from his bed watching him. Maybe willing him to open his eyes. To wake up.

Cristiano is alive. Battered and bruised, his hearing comes and goes but he's alive. The blast had knocked him out. For a minute, I thought he was gone, really gone this time, but he's back.

He looks over at me, stands. I take in the bandages I can see on his arms, his neck, the side of his head and I'm sure he does the same with mine.

But it could be worse.

I glance at Dante.

"You need to let the doctor look at you again," I tell him.

"After." Smears of blood and dirt still stain his clothes and skin. I know most of it isn't his at least.

He takes one of the cups of coffee and leads me to a chair. He sits down beside me, and we watch Dante together.

It's been twenty-seven hours since the house blew up.

Twenty hours since Dante came out of surgery.

I don't know how many hours or days since David kidnapped me.

I look at Cristiano. Neither of us speaks. I think we're just both grateful the other is alive. And worried that Dante may not be for long.

"Did the doctor say anything else?" I ask him. I'd left to get coffee when he'd come in to check Dante's vitals.

"He's sleeping longer than expected. He should have woken up by now."

"Did he say that?"

"Not in so many words but I read between the lines."

"Maybe take what he says at face value, Cristiano."

Cristiano pushes a hand into his hair and gets up, walks to the window. "He's so fucking stubborn."

I follow him and lay my hand on his shoulder. "So are you. Why would you expect he'd be different?"

Dante took the bullet that saved Cristiano's life. It missed his heart by about a centimeter. But that's not all. The blast, the fire, the damage to his right side, his face, body, it's bad.

He sighs deeply. "Some of the families of the women are on their way," Cristiano says, turning back to glance at his brother, unrecognizable beneath the bandages, before shifting his attention to me.

"That's good." Four of the women from the barn made it out alive. Four who are likely to survive out of the dozen. I know I have to focus on the survivors. Be grateful for the four. It's hard, though. Unfair.

"Felix was long gone when we got there. On a flight back to Mexico."

"He's a coward."

He nods in agreement. "How did Mara look?"

"Scared. But brave. She's tough. Still rebellious after ten years. That's something, right?"

He smiles. "It's something."

"There was this woman, Helga. She must have been a sort of horrible nanny-jailor to her. When she," I pause momentarily, not quite sure how to say the next part. "When she died, Mara went through her pockets and stole a switchblade. And a candy bar." I leave out the strap that I'm sure was used to keep her in line. That's not going to do anyone any good to know.

"A candy bar?" He smiles.

I nod. "She's smart, Cristiano. When she met

Petrov she didn't cower, not for a second. And she made him promise to not let Felix hurt me."

"Why?"

"Well...I killed Helga. She didn't just die. I did it."

He nods, pulls me in for a hug. His big hand cradles the back of my head. "That's my Fury."

"Not Little Kitten anymore?"

He draws back, looks down at me, dips his head to kiss me. "Both. You're strong when you need to be and soft when you want to be." He pulls me in for a hug again and rests his chin on the top of my head. "Tell me about the promise she extracted from Felix and Petrov."

"Petrov offered her a gift and she asked that the gift be my safety. He twisted the words around though after he promised I wouldn't be hurt. Felix, too, twisted the words. But when they left, she didn't seem beaten. I think she felt good about having done something to help me. Or thinking she had. Felix knew she wasn't Elizabeth and I know she knows the truth, too. Maybe they sold her to Petrov as Elizabeth Grigori?"

"She'd have been more valuable."

I told him what David told me on the helicopter. That David had arranged for Elizabeth to be kidnapped and sold once she was older. And he told me what David had told them about his mother. About how David suggested his mother had accused him of raping her.

The massacre was his vengeance for her having chosen Cristiano's father over him. For her not loving him back. I wonder if punishing her daughter like he planned to, kidnapping and selling her, if that was also to punish Cristiano's mother or if it was simple economics. Money. Why waste a warm body?

He also told me about Dante, about him possibly being a product of rape. He's already sent DNA to a lab for a paternity test. We're waiting on the results.

"Petrov has disappeared. Charlie thinks he'd arranged the explosives to detonate after he left." I'd assumed the explosions were from Cristiano's men, a distraction, but this makes much more sense.

"Why would he have done that?"

Cristiano shrugs a shoulder. "Maybe he knew Felix and his fondness for cameras? Maybe he just hated the assholes present? Who knows? Who cares?"

"Who is he?"

"Russian businessman. That's all I've been able to get so far. But I'll find him."

"*We* will find him," says a low, raspy voice from the bed.

I gasp, turn my head. Cristiano is beside the bed in an instant.

"Brother!"

A doctor and two nurses rush in. They must have been alerted by the machines to Dante's waking.

"Well, it's good to see you're awake, Mr. Grigori," the doctor says, smiling.

"I'd have opened my eyes earlier but these two were declaring their undying love and I thought I might puke."

We all smile even though I know they all hear the effort it's taking Dante. Even though we all see the extent of the damage.

"I'm glad to see you haven't lost your sense of humor," Cristiano says but there's an edge to his voice, relief but not quite. Dante isn't out of the woods just yet.

The doctor takes a few minutes looking him over and the nurse adjusts his bed so he's sitting up a little. I can see it's painful.

I see his eyes move to me through the holes in the bandages around his head. "Are you okay?"

"I'm in better shape than you."

It's quiet. "How bad?" he asks.

"You're alive. We'll deal with the rest," Cristiano says. "You step between me and a bullet ever again I will fucking kill you myself, do you understand me?"

"You're welcome," Dante says with what I think is a strained chuckle.

"Thank you but don't do it again."

"Mara?"

"She's alive. That's more than we had a few days ago. Like you said, we'll find her. You get yourself healed and out of here and we'll go get her."

"She must be terrified. All these years she's been out there on her own," Dante says.

"I was telling your brother that she's strong. Tough." I leave everything else out.

He nods. "Felix?" he asks Cristiano.

"Back to his hole."

"I'm going to kill that son of a bitch."

"You're going to have to get in line. And you're going to have to get out of here first."

"I want to go home, Brother." He glances out the window at the gray sky, the rain streaking the glass. "This place doesn't agree with me."

"As soon as the doctor gives you the okay, we leave. I've already arranged for doctors—"

"How bad?" Dante asks.

"You've got your arms and legs, you're fucking alive."

He moves an arm, fingers touching the bandages wrapped around his head. "What do I look like?"

"I don't have a mirror," Cristiano lies. He'd made the nurse take out the single mirror in the bathroom just in case.

Dante is quiet, eyes on his brother. He understands. Nods. "Fuck. That stink. Have you had a shower?" he asks Cristiano.

"Fuck you," Cristiano says as his phone rings. He looks at the display. "It's Charlie." He walks toward the door to step into the hallway but stops a moment later and turns to me with a wide smile on his face.

"That's great news. Just a minute." He looks at me. "We found Noah."

I gasp, smile. "Where is he?" But then my mood darkens. "Is he okay?"

"He's fine. He recognized one of my men at the square in Naples."

"So, he found you?" my eyebrows rise up on my forehead. So much for my brother disappearing like he promised. For the first time, I'm glad he didn't listen to me.

"I guess so. He's on the island now. You can call him when I'm done." He excuses himself so it's just Dante and me in the room.

There's an awkward moment of silence before Dante speaks. "I'm sorry I let David take you. I'm sorry for the way I've been to you."

"You were protecting your brother. I know that."

"Still. I'm sorry, Scarlett. You didn't deserve anything you've had to deal with. I know that. I knew it all along."

Warm tears fill my eyes. "It's forgotten. Just get better so we can go home."

Home.

We both smile.

EPILOGUE 1
CRISTIANO

Eight weeks later and Scarlett and I are back home. I moved Dante into a private facility where they can deal with the burns. Cerberus won't leave Scarlett's side.

When we told Lenore about Mara, she was momentarily beside herself happy. But only momentarily. Because she understands the kind of life Mara could be living. The life she'd have been made to endure to survive as long as she has.

I visit Dante daily. I think his singular task—no, his obsession—is keeping him from depression. Maybe keeping him alive.

Find Mara. Bring her home.

He was her protector when she was little and I'm worried about him. Maybe because he's like I was about Marcus Rinaldi. Like I was before Scarlett.

"He's just a big softie," Scarlett says as I shove Cerberus out of our bedroom.

The dog is reluctant to leave and I hear him settle down directly outside the door.

"That's exactly the opposite of his training," I say, turning back to my wife. I look her over. She looks good. She looks happy, brushing out her long, dark hair. She's wearing a soft lilac tank top and matching sleep shorts. She's put on a couple of pounds finally so she's not all skin and bones.

I walk toward her, pulling my shirt off over my head.

Her smile fades and she puts the brush down.

"I need to talk to you," she says, her tone more serious than I expect.

"After."

She licks her lips when I wrap my arms around her waist. I didn't tell her I know what her uncle did to her. It serves no purpose. I have a feeling she left out some things about Mara, but she probably did it for the same reason.

I look down at her, into her soft caramel eyes. She is so beautiful, my wife.

Walking her backward to the wall, I kiss her, taking her wrists from around my neck and dragging her arms up over her head.

"I don't like these," I say against her mouth, pushing the silk shorts down with one hand. "Skirts and dresses only."

She kisses me back. "I'm not wearing underwear. You like that, don't you?"

I cup her sex, feel the soft hairs that have grown back in since the terrible night of the auction.

"I do. Very much. But I'm still burning any jeans or pants you own."

Her lips stretch into a smile as I kiss her. When I flick a finger over her clit, she gasps into my mouth.

I take her mouth in a deep kiss. Then dip my head to kiss her neck, releasing her arms only to pull the tank top off so she's fully naked. I stand back to look at her, take in her fuller breasts with their darkened, hard nipples.

"Fuck," I say, shaking my head, dropping to my knees before her. This woman, my goddess, my Fury, she deserves to be worshipped. "Spread yourself open for me."

She puts her hands on either side of her lower lips and spreads herself open.

I look at her, at her swollen nub, her glistening pink pussy. I dip my head down and flick my tongue over her hard clit before taking it in my mouth. I need to catch her when her knees buckle as she wraps her hands around my head.

I stand, lift her with me and carry her to the bed. Drawing the blankets down, I lay her back on the pillows and spread her legs open. Feasting first with my eyes, then with my tongue and mouth, I taste every inch of her. Hearing her gasps, her cries, feeling her fingers in my hair, twisting it, curling into it, drawing me to her as she pulls her knees back offering me all of her. She's mine. All mine. And I'll never let her go again.

I dip my head down to taste her again and listen to the sound of my name on her lips as her body jerks, as she fists handfuls of the bedsheets, arching her back, giving me everything.

I stand, draw her to the edge of the bed, wiping the back of my hand across my lips as she watches.

"You taste so fucking sweet. I could eat you for breakfast, lunch and dinner." I push my jeans off, step out of them.

Her gaze drops to my cock. She licks her lips and slips to her knees before me, touches the tip of her pretty little tongue to me.

"Fuck," I mutter as she wraps her lips around the head and sucks just a little. Just enough. "That's so good. So fucking good." I brush the hair back from her face. She looks up at me and I think about how much I like her mouth on me, how soft and wet, but that's not what I need tonight. I need to be inside her.

I draw back. She groans as I lift her to stand. I bend to kiss her before bending her over the foot of the bed. She keeps her legs spread wide and arches her back.

"You're perfect," I say, dipping my head to lick the

length of her, hole to hole, before straightening, bringing my cock to her entrance.

She looks back at me as I push into her. I slip one hand under her to play with her and lick my thumb before laying it against her back hole.

She likes this, arching her back for more. I'm happy to give it to her and I'm harder as I look at her like this, stretching to take me, offering herself to me. I press my thumb into her, and she lets out a deep moan. I draw out and flip her onto her back before sliding into her again. I lean in for another kiss, all teeth and tongue now as the fucking grows more frantic. Before long, she's moaning against me, clutching me to her as she shatters around me, making me lose control as I lose myself inside her.

When I finally open my eyes, I find her watching me.

A tear slides down the corner of one eye as she cups the back of my head and leans up to kiss me. I think this is ecstasy. Not the orgasm. Not the physical. But this. My wife beneath me, filled up with me, her hands on me, her smile, her tears.

My heart belongs to her. My soul belongs to her. And hers to me.

That's the real ecstasy.

"I love you, Scarlett."

EPILOGUE 2
SCARLETT

We're lying in bed, Cristiano's big arms around me. I'm curled into him, our heads resting on the same pillow.

He's playing with a strand of my hair. I touch his unshaved face, liking the stubble.

"I would be dead if it wasn't for you," he says.

I study him, thinking about what I need to tell him.

"I didn't want to live afterward. I *wanted* to die. Even though I knew it would kill Dante, I just couldn't. But then there you were, and you made me remember things. Made me feel things. Made me care again. Maybe you make me less selfish, Scarlett."

"You've never been selfish, Cristiano."

He shrugs a shoulder.

"I need to tell you something," I start. I take a

breath in and lay on my back to stare up at the ceiling.

He puts a hand on my belly. Slides it up to cup a breast.

"I like this," he says. "I like a little more meat on you."

"Well, I'm glad you think so."

I sit up, put my pillow on my lap.

"What is it?" he asks, all serious when he sees my expression. He sits up too and takes the pillow out of my arms. He takes my hands. "What?"

I bite my lip. "I know it's soon." I don't know how to do this. I've only known for a few days myself. I feel a tear slide down my cheek and turn my head away. But not fast enough, because he turns it back to him and wipes the tear away.

"Whatever it is, it's fine. We'll figure it out together."

I put a hand to my mouth and look at him. What if...

"I missed my period a couple of weeks ago," I blurt before I can chicken out.

His forehead wrinkles and he looks confused.

"I mean, I've been off anyway with all the stress for so long, so it wasn't a big deal. Honestly I wasn't even paying attention, considering."

"What are you saying?"

"When I was out with Noah the other day, I picked up a test."

I think he stops breathing then. His body goes stock-still.

"A pregnancy test."

His throat works as he swallows.

"There were two in the pack and well, I took the first one and I thought it was wrong because…I mean, it's not like…"

"What are you saying?

"So I took the second one and that one, too…"

"Scarlett?"

I feel myself crying now. Shit. It's not that I'm sad. Not at all. It's just so unexpected.

"I was at the doctor earlier today. That's why I made a big deal of going into town alone."

Cristiano's eyes intensify their gaze on me as he studies me. I'm pretty sure I've never seen him speechless.

"Are you okay?" I ask him.

"Say it."

I study him, search his eyes. "I'm pregnant."

It's quiet. Like dead silent. I stare up at him and he stares back at me.

"Cristiano?"

He blinks, shakes his head, exhales audibly and smiles. Shakes his head again.

"I want to keep it and if you're not ready, I understand. I mean, I get if you—"

He laughs out loud, eyes so bright they make

mine fill up with tears. He's happy. He lifts me and hugs me so hard, I'm sure he's bruised a rib.

"Oh, Scarlett." He draws back to look at me, then hugs me again. "Scarlett. Fuck. Scarlett."

"You're hurting me a little."

He softens his hold, looks at me again, kisses my mouth and pushes the hair back from my face.

"Say it again."

"We're going to have a baby."

Again, he laughs, shakes his head, exhales, shakes his head. Then he lays me down, looks at me, at my belly. It's still flat but he lays his hand on it.

"It's early. I don't think you'll see—"

"We're going to have a baby?"

I nod, still crying because his eyes have filled up too. He lifts me again, hugging me tight.

"We're going to have a baby," he repeats.

"Yes." I'm surprised by his reaction although I didn't know what to expect. "Are you...happy?"

He throws his head back and laughs before his expression grows serious again. He takes my face in his hands, kisses my mouth, keeps hold of me.

"Am I happy? My God, woman. Don't you see how happy I am? How happy you make me?"

I hug him this time, sniffling a little. "I love you so much."

He draws back and takes my face in his hands again, using his thumbs to wipe away tears. "No more tears,

Scarlett. No more fucking tears. I love you and we're going to fill this house up with a dozen babies. Fill it up with laughter again, like it should always have been."

He kisses me.

The end

I hope you enjoyed Scarlett and Cristiano's story and would consider leaving a review at the store where you purchased the book.
Keep reading for a sample of *Requiem for the Soul!*

WHAT TO READ NEXT
REQUIEM OF THE SOUL BY NATASHA KNIGHT AND A. ZAVARELLI

I drift in and out of sleep. My old bed feels foreign, too small tucked up against the wall, the deep pink gauze draping it too childish. I reach out a hand and touch it, remember how I used to like it. Used to pretend I was a princess in a tower.

Wind whistles in from the window I opened to air out the room. The curtain billows, filtering the light coming in from the lamp in the garden. I watch the shadows that dance on the far wall. Remember how I would do that when I was little too. I see figures there, ominous always. The branches of the tree outside make for an eerie gathering as my eyes close again.

I don't know if I drift off for a minute or an hour but when I wake again, it's because of the rain. It's hammering the window. I need to close it, or mom will be angry. Water damage. Like she cares about the house.

I rub my face and untangle myself from the blankets to sit up. I'm momentarily dizzy but that's always the case when I first sit up, so I just close my eyes until the wave passes. But then I hear an unfamiliar rustle then the window giving way as it's pushed closed.

Confused I open my eyes and almost jump out of my skin at the sight that greets me.

There at the window is a figure. Tall and dark and wearing robes like the Grim Reaper.

But the Grim Reaper wouldn't be worried about a little rain getting into the house.

I almost scream as it—he—straightens, turns toward me. I push my back to the wall.

The figure is in a black cloak with a wide hood pulled up over his head so the little bit of light coming in from outside doesn't illuminate his face. The cloak reaches the floor and he's tall. Well over six feet.

I want to scream. I want to open my mouth and scream for help but when I do, nothing comes. No, a sound more pathetic that nothing.

Am I dreaming? Is this a dream, a nightmare I'm trapped in?

But some part of my brain remembers that it knows these robes. Ceremonial. My father had worn one once. I'd been terrified when I'd seen him too.

We remain like that neither he nor I moving, me not even breathing. He has an advantage. He can see my face. See my terror. I can't see his.

Him.

It's a man. His height and build give that away. More reason to scream if only sound would come. Where is my brother now when I need him?

I stare wide-eyed as he takes a step toward me and when he does, the light just touches his face. But it's even more terrifying then because he's wearing a black half-mask and what I glimpse of his face is impossible.

"Wh...what—"

"Ivy Moreno."

Cold, bony fingers seem to crawl along my spine at the deep tenor of his voice and I visibly shudder. The devil's touch. It's what Sister Mary Anthony used to say when that happened. I make the sign of the cross. Habit.

That makes him laugh. It's an ugly laugh. Short and unamused and hard.

I rub my eyes wanting to wake up but when I open them again, he's still there. Closer even.

"How do you know my name?"

"You don't remember me, Ivy? I didn't make an impression? I'm offended."

"I...I don't—"

"You'll be my wife," he continues as if I hadn't stammered my feeble attempt at a response. "It would be strange if I didn't know your name, don't you think?"

His *wife*?

I peer closer. This is Santiago De La Rosa? Why is he wearing that cloak? The mask? It's for ceremonial purposes only. Worn by the founding family members. Males only. And only when tradition dictates it. They'd lent my father a similar cloak when he'd attended one such event. I still remember his excitement even when my sister and I had been terrified to see him in it.

But there's a more pressing question. What the hell is Santiago De La Rosa doing in my room at two in the morning?

Then I remember hearing Abel out in the hallway at some point this night. I remember being irritated that he was making so much noise he'd woken me.

Did Abel let him in here?

"What do you want?" I ask.

I can just make out how his eyes roam over me and I look down at myself. I'm wearing a T-shirt and panties, one foot up on the bed, the other dangling off it. I pull both in, gather up the blankets.

"No need for that," he says, stepping closer still to take the edge of the blanket and tug it slightly off me. "I came to give you something."

I press harder against the wall when he steps to

the edge of the bed. He takes a moment to look at the ornate frame, all the pink.

"A bit childish, isn't it?"

"What do you want with me?"

He looks down at me and I don't know if I see or imagine a grin. Don't know if I imagine the skeleton that peers closer as I back into the corner.

"Oh, that's no way to behave with your husband-to-be, sweet Ivy." He sits on the edge of the bed, inches closer.

"What do you want?" I scream it thinking surely Abel will come. Surely someone will help me.

But nothing. No one comes. I am alone with this man.

He exhales like he's disappointed, then reaches out, touches the tips of his fingers to my cheek, slips them to my neck where my pulse beats wildly.

I keep the back of my head pressed to the wall.

I'm dreaming. I must be. But he feels so real.

"What do you want?" I ask, this time in a quieter voice, a frightened one.

"I already told you that," he starts, voice low and deep.

He takes my hand, his fingers like a vise around it and pulls it toward him. His touch is ice-cold. Maybe it is the Grim Reaper after all.

"I have something for you."

He stretches out my hand, reaches into his

pocket then, as I watch in shocked silence, he forces a ring onto my finger.

"What—"

It's too tight but he doesn't stop until he gets it past the knuckle, the ring icier than his finger.

"There." He releases me.

I pull my hand back and look at it. At the large teardrop-shaped dark stone on my finger. At the skeleton like fingers that seem to hold the huge rock in place. Like bones. I glance at him then instantly try to pry it off.

"It's no use," he says, watching me.

I still try. I don't want this. I don't want any of it. And when he moves to stand, I swear I see that smile again. A dead man's smile.

I feel blood drain from my head, my vision fading as the room begins to spin.

"You belong to me now, Ivy Moreno, for better or for worse. Until death do us part."

One-click Requiem of the Soul Now!

ALSO BY NATASHA KNIGHT

The Society Trilogy

Requiem of the Soul

Reparation of Sin

Resurrection of the Heart

To Have and To Hold Duet

With This Ring

I Thee Take

Dark Legacy Trilogy

Taken (Dark Legacy, Book 1)

Torn (Dark Legacy, Book 2)

Twisted (Dark Legacy, Book 3)

Unholy Union Duet

Unholy Union

Unholy Intent

Collateral Damage Duet

Collateral: an Arranged Marriage Mafia Romance

Damage: an Arranged Marriage Mafia Romance

Ties that Bind Duet

Mine

His

MacLeod Brothers

Devil's Bargain

Benedetti Mafia World

Salvatore: a Dark Mafia Romance

Dominic: a Dark Mafia Romance

Sergio: a Dark Mafia Romance

The Benedetti Brothers Box Set (Contains Salvatore, Dominic and Sergio)

Killian: a Dark Mafia Romance

Giovanni: a Dark Mafia Romance

The Amado Brothers

Dishonorable

Disgraced

Unhinged

Standalone Dark Romance

Descent

Deviant

Beautiful Liar

Retribution

Theirs To Take

Captive, Mine

Alpha

Given to the Savage

Taken by the Beast

Claimed by the Beast

Captive's Desire

Protective Custody

Amy's Strict Doctor

Taming Emma

Taming Megan

Taming Naia

Reclaiming Sophie

The Firefighter's Girl

Dangerous Defiance

Her Rogue Knight

Taught To Kneel

Tamed: the Roark Brothers Trilogy

THANK YOU!

Thanks for reading *I Thee Take*. I hope you enjoyed it. Reviews help new readers find books and would make me ever grateful. Please consider leaving a review at the store where you purchased the book.

Click here to sign up for my newsletter to receive new release news and updates!

Like my FB Author Page to keep updated on news and giveaways!

I have a FB Fan Group where I share exclusive teasers, giveaways and just fun stuff. Probably TMI :) It's called The Knight Spot. I'd love for you to join us! Just click here!

ABOUT THE AUTHOR

Natasha Knight is the *USA Today* Bestselling author of Romantic Suspense and Dark Romance Novels. She has sold over half a million books and is translated into six languages. She currently lives in The Netherlands with her husband and two daughters and when she's not writing, she's walking in the woods listening to a book, sitting in a corner reading or off exploring the world as often as she can get away.

Write Natasha here: natasha@natasha-knight.com

Click here to sign up for my newsletter to receive new release news and updates!

NATASHA KNIGHT

www.natasha-knight.com
natasha-knight@outlook.com

Printed in Great Britain
by Amazon